My Perfect Family

MY PERFECT FAMILY

ADRIANE LEIGH

JOFFE BOOKS

Revised edition 2024
Joffe Books, London
www.joffebooks.com

First published in the USA in 2020 as *Before She Lied*

This paperback edition was first published
in Great Britain in 2024

Cover art by Nick Castle

ISBN: 978-1-83526-713-4

PROLOGUE

Death.

Sweet in its finality, peaceful if planned well.

I flipped the glossy polaroid in my hand, the toothless grin of Tommy Monroe staring back at me.

I never imagined I'd find myself here, lingering at the edges of the woods, waiting for a life to be snuffed out. But fate had other plans, my calling clear as the warm months spun to autumn.

I'd bided my time, watching and waiting, knowing soon the day would come where I would have the last laugh. Too many wrongs needed righting, revenge sharper than the taste of blood on my tongue.

I tucked the small photo in my pocket when I heard a scream on the wind. Darkness drew long shadows across the boat dock as I heard shouts and cries coming closer.

Tucking myself deeper into the treeline, I waited patiently under the boughs of a giant evergreen, the feathery tips caressing the murky water at my feet.

I heard footsteps hit the dock then, running quickly and shuttling fast in my direction as a baby's cry pierced the night air.

Danger lurked around the Point, its residents willfully in the dark.

I pressed tighter against the tree bark as the figure turned the corner on the dock and sped past the boathouse. Tommy Monroe's terrified cries cracked my eardrums.

I heard a soft scuffle, then the urgent rowing of oars slicing through the water as they pulled away from the dock. The small boy's cries were quieter now, the gentle rocking of the bay lulling him into a false sense of security.

Anticipation mixed with adrenaline as I wondered when anyone would next see them again.

A mother's shriek lit my ears a moment later.

The moment.

Her footsteps pounded down the deck boards, my heart rate spiking as I imagined what would happen next.

Sweet relief, the only destination.

"Tommy!" Lennox Monroe stopped at the railing, violent pants racking her small form. She seemed to be debating something.

Soon, peace will find them. All of them.

Just as she squared her shoulders and seemed about to launch herself off the deck and into the black water, a hooded figure stepped out of the shadows and swung for her head.

The crushing *thunk* of metal meeting skull flooded my veins with a giddy sensation.

The soft *snick snick* of a body being pulled across wood came next, before I heard the solid thud as it was flipped into the hull of a boat.

The soft rumble of an engine cut through the mist then, and the boat motored away as I pulled the hat from my jacket pocket. The rough woolen fibers were abrasive against my fingertips. The vibrant yellow threads were just the right shade to stand out in the inky black night.

I tossed the baby's hat into the black water and walked down the winding path that led away from the shoreline with a renewed spring in my step.

Step one was complete.
Finally, our chance had come.
Finally.
Rebirth.
The fun had just begun.

CHAPTER ONE

Morrissey

"Tommy!" Lennox called through the house in that sing-song tone I loved so much.

I ducked my head in the kitchen, smiling when my son tossed a fistful of cereal from the perch of his highchair. "What's up, little man? Makin' Mommy crazy bananas again?"

Tommy banged both open palms on his tray, drool decorating his chubby cheeks. He pursed his lips, a frowny face crossing his forehead. I laughed and he seemed to like it, two tiny front teeth grinning back at me.

"He needs a bath and I'm on deadline with this Pumpkin Fest fundraiser at the academy. If I don't finish it, the board chair will have my head."

"Lenn — it's a charity bake auction, just send an email and ask everyone to pick up some cupcakes."

She wiped his face with a napkin. "It's never as easy as you men think, you know." She tapped my nose with the pad of her index finger and then pressed a tender kiss to my lips. "If I don't hand deliver this design to the newspaper, I'm cooked, Monroe. And trust me, you don't want to pick up those pieces."

I laughed. "Whatever you say, baby. How late does Carl stay at that place anyway?"

"He said he'd be there 'til ten. He's writing a piece about a cold case from across the bay. Someone from one of those little fishing villages, I think. Hopefully he doesn't keep me too long tonight, I'm exhausted already."

"Okay, if you stay late, send me a text. I'll probably hit the hay early, I've got that charter over to the island first thing in the morning to deliver supplies. I should be home before you're even awake though." I lifted Tommy out of his high-chair and held him up. "I'll give this little monster a bath and have him all tucked up in no time, snug as a bug in a rug."

"Thank you, baby." My wife raised up on her tiptoes and placed a kiss on our son's cheek before patting his head. "I put cinnamon rolls in the fridge for morning. If you get home from your flight early enough tomorrow there might be one or two left for you."

"I'll rush home. I wouldn't miss your homemade cinnamon rolls for the world."

She gathered up her big work bag as I held Tommy, shoving a manilla folder inside. I followed her to the front door, one last grin turning up her cheeks as she turned back to us. "Both of my men, so handsome. I love you so much."

I bounced my boy on my hip, forcing a small smile on his face. "We'll have buckets of fun. He's a little water baby, just like his mama."

"Don't forget his bedtime story."

"I know, I know."

"Don't have too much fun without me!"

I gave her an easy smile before we both waved her off, solid wooden doors closing with a resounding thunk behind her. I heard the security alarm beep once, ensuring that it was activated, before glancing at the tiny motion-sensor camera overlooking the front gate. I saw her reverse from the garage in the background, lights glowing brighter as she came closer to the gate in her Audi SUV, obscuring the camera with the sleek black finish for a moment before passing again as the gate opened and she turned south down Smokey Hollow Road.

The autumn sun was already past setting, the darkness outside enveloping the rolling grounds of our estate on the bay. We didn't need a place so big for just the three of us, but we enjoyed the hell out of our little slice of Heaven.

We'd lucked out when the foreclosed property came on the market. It was modern and rambling, a two-story contemporary home sandwiched on a tiny thumb of land jutting between two turquoise Lake Michigan bays. Unique with its white stucco walls and Aegean-blue trim and roof, it was "fit for a Greek getaway," our realtor had said. It was our dream home, and even at foreclosed cost, it was at the maximum end of our budget, but I'd seen the way my wife's eyes lit up when she saw this property for the first time.

My offer was accepted within twenty-four hours, and we moved in the same week of our wedding. By the time we'd welcomed our beautiful boy into the world, we'd settled into our quiet life up on the hill. The 4,000-square-foot home with finished basement living area was far more space than we needed, but around us sprawled rolling vineyards, watery vistas and the iconic Castle Rock Lighthouse in the distance.

Thieves Cove was the perfect place to raise a family. Or at least it had been.

Industry had left the town when I was a kid, meaning tourism was the only economic support left to our secluded neck of the Great Lakes. Lennox and I had grown up just miles apart, but never came much into contact with each other previous to the summer before we left for college.

She'd charmed me with her beauty and dry sense of humor, always pulling me feet first into every best adventure of my life. I didn't know what being alive was until Lennox McGregor came along.

"So whaddya say? If we make this bath quick, we have some ice cream and sprinkles for dessert."

Drool leaked down the side of his cheek as he chewed on one chubby finger.

"Ice cream?" I bounced him on my hip again as I watched the gates close and lock behind Lennox before Tommy and I drifted down the hallway to the bathtub adjacent to his nursery. "Can you say ice cream?"

More drool tumbled. I shook my head, wiping at his little pink lips with a smile that only this kid could bring to my face.

"I know Mommy usually does your baths, but tonight it's just the guys." I began unwrapping him from the layers of trendy clothes Lennox always dressed him in. "Tonight—" I tossed his diaper in the pail at my side — "is bro time."

He babbled happily.

"Dadda. Can you say Dadda?" I set him on the white tile floor, naked as the day he was born. He chewed on one finger and pointed, tiny tufts of dark hair whispering across his formerly bald little head that made me already want to squeeze him to my chest and make him promise to never grow up.

Tommy pointed to the bathroom.

"Bathtub. Can you say bathtub?"

He was content to jabber as I flipped the water on and let the tub fill up. "Bubbles?"

I handed him the bottle of organic kids' bubble bath and he took it from me quickly and whipped it to the floor. "Okay, not manly enough, I don't disagree. Ready to get in the water?"

Tommy wiggled his fat little feet. I couldn't help the laugh, lifting him into the warmth and watching as he sank down into his upright bath chair, the suction of the foam material holding him firmly in place while he splashed and played. The water rolled around his little feet and he squealed with delight.

I tossed him a few yellow rubber duckies to play with and he gathered them all in his hands, frustrated when he couldn't hold them all at once like he wanted. We played bumper cars with the duckies and that cheered him up, distracting him enough that when the water was past his little belly button, I shut off the tap and let him splash in the few inches of water.

"You keep playing, I'll be right back, I'm just going to turn on the sports update for my fantasy football." He wasn't even listening, those rubber duckies occupying all of his time.

Firmly seated in his foam bath chair, I knew he was safe to splash to his heart's content without falling or slipping into the shallow bath water.

I darted out of the bathroom and around the corner into the master bedroom, flicking on the television to find *Sports Center* still on from last night. I cranked the commentary a little louder so I could hear over all the duckie bumper car splashing we were doing, and then swiped my phone and eyeballed the updates of the scores for the other guys in my fantasy league. I came around the corner, eyes on my phone and not on my feet, when I knocked into a bag at the edge of our bed.

I groaned once, ready to kick it back under the bed, when I realized an old file folder from when we'd bought the house had fallen out. Lennox must have pulled it out in her stack while in search of manilla folders to use for the bake auction project. I dropped to my knees, swooping the folder up with the mortgage paperwork inside and our bank's logo emblazoned on the top. I stuffed it in my nightstand so Tommy wouldn't latch onto it and drool all the important details away, and then bent further in search of any other stray paperwork that might have fallen or been shoved under the bed.

I flipped on the flashlight on my phone, sweeping it under the bed slowly as I squinted, searching for anything out of the ordinary. Only a thousand and one dust bunnies greeted me. Maybe I'd leave a note on the fridge to order a new file cabinet come morning. Lennox had been complaining last week about the lock on the old one going haywire. I'd chalked it up to rust from all the humidity that lingered between the two bodies of water that landlocked our estate.

Tommy's babbling bolted me from my thoughts and sent me flying around the corner into the bathroom. He beamed up at me, two rubber duckies in his hands and another perched on the top of his head.

"Look at the talent already on you." I clapped my hands and made a little show of dancing around the bathroom and he erupted into giggles, rubber duckie toppling.

He scooped it and began blabbering in gibberish as I soaped up his tiny puff of hair with shampoo and then his body with the organic wash. Five minutes later and he was wrapped in his favorite duckie towel, diaper fastened around his little waist, and we were snacking on a few bites of ice cream straight from the freezer.

Me and my boy.

I never thought much of having children, but Lennox had always been dead set on family life. I loved her for it then, and I loved her even more now. I was never a romantic guy, but I was lucky because Lennox never asked that of me — if she had, I would have disappointed her. But I did my best to tell her how much I loved her, then and now. I could see the strain motherhood cast on her usually vibrant green eyes. She was so impossibly strong through the difficult pregnancy with Tommy, and I'd never dreamed I could love two people so much.

"Okay, little water baby, whaddya say we brush those little chompers and go night-night now?"

He began squealing, vanilla goo splattered on his face and his little fists shaking in the air. I slipped the carton back in the freezer and took Tommy back to the bathroom, where we brushed his teeth and he fought with the toothbrush before he began chewing on it to relieve his teething gums.

"I wonder if Mama has been putting you to bed with teething medicine?" I wondered out loud, searching for the tiny bottle Lennox had been keeping on the counter of late. "Maybe she used all of it up on you last night, huh?"

I slipped his toothbrush back in the drawer, then brought him to the crib in the nursery. As soon as I tucked him in, little blanket around his little shoulders, he shot up and screamed, arms flailing in the air.

"Yikes, okay, maybe a nursery rhyme or something?" I tucked him back in, picking up the small book of goodnight rhymes at the table next to his crib. He was already on his feet, watery eyes on mine.

I tried to tuck him back in with his blanket. It was hopeless, so instead I settled myself in the chair with the rhymes and let him climb into my lap. I tucked his little head under my chin and we began to read together. First one nursery rhyme, then two, and then the entire book. By the time I flipped the last page, his eyes were thankfully a little heavier than they'd been.

Static crackled to life on the baby monitor, waking Tommy up and causing his little arms to thrust out. I huffed, swaying him back to sleep while humming softly. I neared the crib again and the monitor crackled to life. I realized the signal from my cell phone coming within range of the monitor was probably setting it off. I tucked Tommy in, careful to straighten his blanket just like Lennox had instructed me over and over. I breathed a sigh of relief as I walked out the door, leaving the nursery door open a crack before padding into the master bedroom. I turned *Sports Center* to low, turned the monitor on the nightstand to a higher volume so I could hear him if he tried to crawl out again, and then headed for a hot shower.

I was just rinsing the soap suds out of my hair when I heard Tommy blabbering in his crib, his tiny voice echoing through the master bathroom and loud enough to hear over the spray of the shower.

He was chanting some gibberish on repeat. I ducked out of the shower and wrapped myself in a towel, thinking he sounded fairly happy. When I reached the monitor on the counter, I tapped the screen, trying to get the video to come to life. The video flickered a few times, then died out totally. I could still hear him cooing softly, rustling around his little blanket and pillow, but with every babble he was sounding groggier again, and I could just imagine him drifting off into the land of nod.

He was an active little guy, there was no doubt about it. Getting him to go to sleep had been a chore from the beginning. I smiled to myself, confident when he finally settled down and the monitor went silent. I set it back on the counter, flopped myself on the master bed, and was sound asleep before I'd even remembered to turn off the game stats.

CHAPTER TWO

Lennox
Three summers ago — June

"Morrissey Monroe, you're insane! Stop, stop!" My shriek rang through the air; his hands, freezing cold from the icy water, were flailing and causing spray to land on the line of girls watching by the dock.

Jenny, Carl's seventeen-year-old sister, launched herself into the lake, crying bloody murder and locking her arms around her brother's neck to pretend to drown him. Just watching them play fight sent a shiver down my spine. I didn't realize how much I'd missed my high school crew until I was home from college — I'd only just completed my second year at Central, less than two hours away — and Morrissey had transferred to school with me, despite the fact that his dad wanted him to go to business school at U of M before taking over the transport company someday. He'd stayed close to home for me though.

We'd all turned twenty-one this year and life couldn't be better.

"Come out for a skinny dip, ladies. Don't be shy now." Kel waved to our small group on shore, winking at Jenny before stripping his trunks off and throwing them up in the air.

"He was raised by animals," I laughed.

"Nope, just the fine sheriff of our little cove."

Kel swam closer, threatening to stand up and give everyone a view of his birthday suit. "I got the charm from my grandma."

"Trust me, his grandma is more savage than his dad."

"Never knew my mom, doesn't it make you want to fix me?" He exaggerated his puppy dog eyes and waggled his eyebrows. "I've got a million mommy issues."

Morrissey kicked water at his best friend.

Kel ignored him, laying the comedy on thicker. "In fact, my dad and Lenn's mom dated in high school." Kel swam closer to me. "Imagine how things could have been different between us."

I kicked both of my feet, creating a wave to keep him at bay. "I don't know if I'm the one that's lucky or you."

"Come swim and I'll forget it ever happened."

"You haven't let me live it down since you found out they dated!"

"Whatcha afraid of? You were practically born on the water."

My body stiffened, eyes flicking up to the clear sky.

"Come on, Lenn — I'll protect you." Morrissey's palms settled on my bare knees. My feet dangled as I shook my head.

"Nope and thanks," I hummed. "I'm happy right here."

"But you go swimming in my pool all the time." Morrissey tilted his head to one side, eyebrow arching.

"That's different."

"We won't let a sturgeon bite your toes, Lenn!" Carl called from the water, Jenny already looking chilled to the bone through her racerback swimsuit. She was a year younger than the rest of us, but the strongest swimmer by far. She'd been butterfly stroking her way to championships since she was in middle school, smoking all of us in laps in Morrissey's family pool easily. I envied her courage and stamina. I loved to swim, but not in the big lake. Never in the big lake.

"It's not the sturgeons I'm worried about!" I called back.

"We won't let Morris bite you either!" Kel called, and then threw a soaked nerf ball at Morrissey's back.

He turned, fetching the football and whipping it back full force. The velocity of his throw sprayed all of us up on the dock again.

"Someday I wanna live here."

"Newsflash, Lennox, you already do." Jenny unwrapped a sucker with a bubblegum center and started chomping on it.

"Suckers—" I snagged another from the stash in her bag — "are so last summer."

"Go off to college and suddenly you're too good for suckers?" She rolled her eyes.

"Definitely too good for those fools." I kicked water toward Kel and Carl, still throwing the football back and forth in the water.

"We're all too good for those fools," Jenny laughed. "Besides, I thought you wanted to get out of here someday, that's what Carl always said."

"Hm, maybe not anymore." My eyes trailed across the turquoise waves that lapped the shore of the bay. "Not if I could live here, right here. Right out on the Point with a view of the lighthouse. I think I could live here then. But if staying in Thieves Cove means livin' on the edge of town in the mobile park, I'll pass."

Morrissey tilted his head up to me then, a smile curling up before he lifted himself straight out of the water and leaned over, catching my lips in a kiss. "You'll stay if I ask you to marry me."

I laughed awkwardly. "I don't see *I do's* in my future anytime soon, Morrissey Monroe."

"You say that now." He kissed me once again before sliding back into the water and swimming back through the waves to meet the guys on the shallow sandbar.

"Fools, all of them. It's freezing cold out there; I think I saw an iceberg in the distance," I quipped.

I laughed, more thankful for every year of independence I had from my family. I'd never spent much time on the Point before meeting Morrissey and Kel. Carl, Jenny and I had grown up just a few households down from each other, but Morrissey and Kel came from the better side of town.

Kel's dad was the sheriff and Morrissey's parents were another level entirely. His dad owned a private charter company, Titan Transport, operating by boat, plane, and road to get supplies out to the inhabitants of some of the smaller islands offshore. His parents had done well; the sprawling fifty-acre estate they lived on was gated and they hired a full-time maid to take care of the daily household chores.

Morrissey's mom ran a successful counseling center that kept her away even more than his dad's work, so Morrissey was home alone a lot. We played video games and swam in the pool and talked about the cheerleaders we hated and the football players that chased them.

I'd never felt like I fit anywhere, until Morrissey Monroe wrapped me up in his arms.

"Have you seen that big mansion up on the Point?" Jenny dipped her toes in the water again, bringing me back from my wandering thoughts.

"Mansion?"

"Yeah, the road we came in on, if you keep going another mile or so the trees open up and there's a big sprawling mansion called the Hollows, way bigger than Morrissey's house. It's gated with a boathouse and dock and it sits up on a little bluff that overlooks the lighthouse. It's the prettiest thing I've ever seen. My dad drove us up here to sell Girl Scout cookies one time because he said he was sick and tired of our neighbors not paying us for the orders. They never answered, so we'll never know. But I loved that house, I still remember it. It's one of those places that you can't unsee, you know?"

"Yeah," I breathed, wondering what it would be like to live in a house like that someday. The kind of house that made everyone talk.

Morrissey pulled me into the water then, distracting my thoughts and holding me close to him so it never lapped higher than the backs of my knees.

"Please don't let me go," I begged, terror building inside of me.

"Never, Lenn. Never."

A shriek pulled our attention from each other then — a bunch of bikini-clad tourist girls were rowing out toward Kel and Carl. It was only minutes before Kel had tipped their boat and sent them screaming into the bay, bobbing and splashing and tackling each other in the waves.

By the time the sun had set over the water, the shadows of the evergreens along Smokey Hollow Road loomed large along the shoreline.

"Kel looks pretty serious about that tourist girl," I whispered.

Morrissey only chuckled as Kel tossed another bottle of beer over his shoulder. It crashed on the stones and lapped at the water's edge. Morrissey shook his head, standing to clean up his best friend's mess. "He may be older than me but that doesn't make him smarter."

"Older than you?"

"He's a year and a half older, but his dad and grandma held him back a year in grade school."

"Really?" I laughed. "I thought the police academy would have whipped him into something a little more respectable by now."

"Police academy? He's already graduated. He walked into the Thieves Cove department as a deputy because of his last name."

Morrissey shrugged, gathering up all of the beer bottles the group had left on the beach.

"I should get back to the campground," the last tourist girl mumbled drunkenly as she and Kel approached the shore. Her legs were wrapped around his body, lips against his neck.

"Don't leave yet."

"My parents will send a search party for me."

"Kel, she's got to go home, man. You don't need any more trouble with the tourist girls."

"Don't worry about it." Kel waved Morrissey off. "I missed the pretty tourist girls while I was at the academy. Give me this, bro." His lips connected to her neck.

"Kel! Let Carl drive her back, he hasn't been drinking as much." Morrissey grabbed Kel's shoulder but Kel pushed him off, his focus only on the girl in his arms.

"Carl already left on his bike, and Jenny won't even ride tandem with him because she said he's drunk cycling."

Morrissey swore under his breath.

Kel didn't miss a beat though, snatching up his shorts with one hand before bringing the tourist girl to his car. Morrissey called into the night air again, but Kel didn't reply, only brought the engine to life on his little sports car and peeled out of the dirt patch parking lot.

"I'd better follow him."

CHAPTER THREE

Morrissey

"Morning, buddy," I said as I entered the nursery, crossing the room to open the floor-to-ceiling curtains. I spread the heavy drapes wide, expecting my boy to be waiting for me as I turned, toothy grin on his sleepy face like most mornings.

Except he wasn't there.

I frowned, stepping closer to the crib to find it empty.

"Tommy?" I dropped to my knees, searching under the crib — maybe he'd crawled out in the middle of the night and couldn't get back in, so he fell asleep somewhere else. Or maybe Lennox had woken up early for a morning walk; she did that a lot of mornings when he was up with the birds.

I left the nursery, popping into our bedroom to make sure she wasn't in there with him and I hadn't realized it. When I found that clear, I hunted through the top floor of the big house, searched the family room and basement below, then swung the main door open so a burst of September air slapped me in the face. I noticed the boots Lennox had worn yesterday, kicked off haphazardly, probably when she'd come home in the middle of the night.

I pushed a hand through my hair, double-checking the garage camera to find her SUV parked as it had been earlier this morning when I'd left for work. I shook my head, wondering where she would have gone in this weather anyway. It was half drizzling with dark clouds hanging over the bay all morning — I'd hardly been able to fly my plane into the Castle Light airstrip to make my delivery.

Because of the fog hanging so low over the water, I'd canceled the rest of my trips scheduled that day and came home early. If the fog burned off early enough, I could always do my runs later, but by the look of things the weather was only about to take a turn for the worse.

My heart started to flip in my chest then, hoping maybe they were in the family room that we never used downstairs, or maybe he was splashing in puddles down by the beach — one of Tommy's favorite hobbies when he wasn't drooling and eating.

I jogged to the stone path that led over the hill and down to the beach. The fog was thicker than cream soup, but my bare feet sped up anyway, fear suddenly locking itself in my mind. "Tommy!"

I began calling on repeat as loudly as I could as I got nearer to the shore. The fog hung heavier, but I could hear the gentle lap of the water before I finally was past my ankles in it. "Tommy!"

I cursed the weather, cursed myself for not having shoes on, for not having a flashlight, for not checking on him when I'd left early this morning before my morning flight. "Lenn!"

I searched frantically up and down the shoreline, raking the edge of the woods, looking among the wet rocks for any sign of them. I ran down the dock to the boathouse; our boat was tucked safely inside and the door securely locked. I searched under the dock pilings, praying I was overreacting and maybe they'd just run to the neighbors because Lennox was out of coffee, or . . .

"Tommy?" I choked on the word when my eye caught a flash of school-bus yellow. I lunged down the shore, drenching myself up to my thighs before catching Tommy's homemade yellow-knit hat.

Terror built up in my veins, my eyes blinking away the horror as I realized what I was looking at.

My wife. My son. *Vanished.*

I ran blindly back to the house and found my phone to call the police department. Somehow, they were on my doorstep before I could register that any of this was even real.

"Morris?" Kel's eyes were still caked with sleep when I buzzed him in the gate three minutes later.

"Tommy is missing."

The speaker was silent, but I could see the shadow of his patrol car on screen. "What do you mean, *Tommy is missing*?"

"Lennox too."

He parked at the front door, and I opened it to meet him at the threshold.

"For how long?" He pulled out a small notepad and scribbled down something.

"I don't know — minutes, hours? Just got home from running food and shit to Castle Rock Island. I assumed they were here when I left. Her car was here, and sometimes she sleeps on the couch in her office when she goes to bed late so she doesn't wake me up before an early morning flight. But I . . . I guess I don't know for sure."

"You don't know?" His eyes were dark with worry. "You gotta give me more than that, man, think about it. Do you know what they were wearing? I can call in an Amber Alert—"

"I, fuck, I . . ." I crushed my palms over my face, searching the tired memory of my mind. "Tommy was only in a diaper when I put him to bed last night. And his blanket, his blanket is gone."

"Okay, what about her?"

I scratched my head, trying to remember exactly what she'd been wearing yesterday. "Jeans, these boots—" I kicked the leather things at the floor next to my feet — "a dark shirt and maybe a puffer vest on top. I just . . . I can't remember."

"Okay, that's good enough. You're sure her car is here? There's no other vehicle she could have taken?"

"No, there's the tractor, but no one's taking that anywhere fast."

"Okay, I'm going to call dispatch and have them submit the alert, and I'll call backup. I'll get a missing persons unit assembled to turn the Point upside down looking for them. We're going to get to the bottom of this, Morrissey, I swear to you."

His eyes held mine as he backed away, his gaze lingering on my bare feet, soaked and caked with lake muck from my morning search. "Wait!"

"Wait!" I spun, grasping Tommy's hat in my fist. It was drenched through, and my hand shook as I followed Kel with it. "This, this is Tommy's, I found it on the beach."

"Down there?" His eyes rose as he gestured down the path to the bay.

"Yeah, near the boathouse. The boat is there though and everything is locked up safely."

"Okay." I could see him visibly swallow before taking a few steps back again and holding his hand out. "Just stay there a minute, let me get this called in."

I squeezed the hat in my fist before I brought it to my nose and inhaled. It smelled like the shampoo I'd used on Tommy last night. My mind flashed back to the moment on the baby monitor when I'd heard him cooing and babbling while I was in the shower. It had seemed normal then, but had it been?

"Okay, a few guys should be up here in a minute. Mind taking a walk with me?"

"A walk?"

"Yeah." His eyes tracked from my face to the garage behind me. "I'd like you to show me where you say you found that hat."

"Oh, of course. Who will buzz your guys in at the gate when they get here?"

"Oh, we'll just be a minute. Or we can leave it open. You've got closed-circuit footage, haven't you? There's no getting in or out of here without a record of it."

I pointed him down the path to where I'd found Tommy's hat.

"Wait, Morrissey?"

"Yeah?" I paused.

"You want to put on some shoes?"

I felt about as helpless as I must have looked. "Yeah." I passed Kel on my way back to the house to grab shoes. "I'm glad it's you that's here with me, buddy, I know you've got my back."

Kel's frown deepened for a moment before he cleared his throat. "Sure, buddy. Anything you need."

CHAPTER FOUR

Lennox
Three summers ago — June

Mist clung to the edges of the dark pavement.

The roar of the Charger echoed through the evergreens as we floated down Smokey Hollow Road, the smell of sand and sun on our skin.

"We just passed the campground."

I could see Morrissey's frown deepening in the moonlight, a classic rock song playing on the radio as he slowed and took another corner, this one tighter.

"The road is slick," he murmured, the edge of his front passenger tire edging off the sharp turn and into the gravel shoulder. He overcorrected the wheel, flinging us back over the median line and causing my heart to hammer.

"You okay?" Morrissey looked across the cab at me.

"Yeah, I'm fine." I breathed, relaxing when he slowed off the gas pedal more, preparing for the next big turn.

We crested the bluff, moonlight breaking through the trees and highlighting the low guard rail and shimmering navy bay beyond.

"Holy shit — is that Kel's car?" The sound of fear sliced his words.

"Is it?" I clutched at the door of the Charger as Morrissey slowed the engine to a creep, only the tail end of a silver fender visible over the lip of the deep road drain. "Oh my God, I bet they've been there for at least an hour!"

I hurled myself out of the Charger and ran for Kel's sports car, shocked when the heavy arms of a stranger circled my torso and yanked me into the thick treeline. The scent of fresh straw filled my nose. "You don't want to see what's in there."

The hands let go of me, the gruff voice still sending a shudder to my toes. Had it even happened at all?

Sirens pierced the night air in the next breath, a patrol car followed by an ambulance and fire truck arriving in quick succession.

"Dad!" Kel screamed wildly, his arm flying out of the driver's side window. "I'm stuck."

We watched as Sheriff Kendry raced to his son, still behind the wheel of the sports car. "Are you okay?"

"Yeah, my leg is pinned."

Paramedics pushed us away from the scene then, working to check Kel's vitals before he waved them off.

"I'm fine, get her out of there though!"

"Her?" His dad leaned in through the broken window then waved for the firefighters. "Bring the saw, boys!"

We watched in silent horror just at the edge of the evergreens as the volunteer fire department cut Kel's unconscious passenger from the car, administering CPR to the young woman before loading her into the ambulance and screaming off into the night. I imagined her parents, here for a relaxing vacation, and now they would spend the rest of their time in Thieves Cove in an emergency room.

By the time she was gone, Kel had been rescued from the car and allowed paramedics to wrap his leg — thigh to knee.

I approached cautiously, my hand in Morrissey's and still shaking, even though the night air wasn't cold.

"Morrissey?" Shock shot across Sheriff Kendry's face. "Did you see what happened?"

"No, sir. We arrived just a few minutes too late." Morrissey glanced at me.

The sheriff ducked around Kel. "Please, that girl is lucky to be alive — tell me, if he's been drinking again—"

"Dad, no, I wasn't!" Kel sounded so young.

"Kel, shut up." He waved his son off. "Tell me, Morrissey, tell me if my son was drunk when he got behind that wheel tonight."

My fingers twitched in Morrissey's when Sheriff Kendry said the words.

"Drunk? No, sir. The pavement was wet back there before the bluff edge; my tires hit a patch and sent me into the shoulder."

"Well, at the bare minimum that's a citation for too fast for conditions," the sheriff gruffed, eyes tracking between Morrissey's and mine now. "Who was that girl?"

"Some tourist girl," Morrissey offered. "We don't even know her name, sir."

CHAPTER FIVE

Morrissey
First day: 4.34 p.m.

"Can I have a minute, Morrissey?" Kel ducked his head into the office. I lifted my head from Lennox's work desk, frown and sleep lines criss-crossing my face.

"Sure." Lenn and Tommy had been missing all day, and Kel and a crew of dozens of uniformed officers had scoured my home in search of my missing family. Kel had dispatched two sheriff's boats to hunt both the east and west bays for clues. What was normally a peaceful place was now a hive of chaos and bodies.

"Don't have any enemies, do you? A rival winemaker across the bay or maybe someone pissed off at Titan?"

"Who isn't pissed off at Titan in this town?"

Kel didn't answer, only scribbled something on his stupid little pad before finally uttering, "I spoke to Lenn's dad this morning, he doesn't look good. Helda must have been over to visit him. He cut up some fresh banana bread and we had coffee and he filled me in on all the medical stuff he's been struggling with lately. He said Helda is so damn worried all she's done is bake bread and delivered it to all the neighbors in the park."

I grinned. Helda's fresh-baked bread was famous in Thieves Cove. "Lenn's dad's been on the transplant list for two years now."

"I hope it works out soon for him. He's on a lot of medication and seemed pretty groggy. I don't think he knows anything about what happened."

"Lenn's been sending him cash every month, and even wanted to refinance the Hollows to try to secure him a kidney, but we haven't exactly built up much equity yet."

"Has Lenn mentioned seeing her mom lately?"

"No, it's been months since she's heard anything, as far as I know," I said. "She sent some things for the baby shower but that's it."

"Just want to make sure." He lingered at the doorway as he spoke. "You said you left around four thirty this morning to make that flight at the hangar, right?"

"Yes." It all felt like a blur. *I could be forgetting and lying to him right now and I'd hardly know it.*

Hours and hours of walking the property, searching for clues. Then bloodhounds and drones and dives of the surrounding bay, just in case . . . just in case the worst had happened.

"Okay, I just want to double-check that with the guys back at the precinct reviewing the security tape."

"I handed it over this morning, they haven't found anything yet?"

He shook his head. "Nothing out of the ordinary. We located several sets of footprints down by the shore — yours barefoot, just like I found you this morning, but others too. Boots from the looks of it, and another set of sneakers. Looks like there's been a lot of action down there. I know it doesn't seem like much, but it's early, these things take time to reveal themselves."

"Time? Aren't the first twenty-four hours the most critical?"

"Sure are, and we've had dozens of officers canvasing this property you got here, from the vineyards down to the shoreline. They haven't found a thing. Now, unless you think they walked off into thin air—"

I waved my hand at him to shut him down, my brain no longer able to process the words or their implications. They'd already turned the house upside down, a member of the tech crew lingering in every room and office, from the basement living area to the rooftop balcony. They'd pulled all of Lenn's clothes out of the walk-in closet, upturned Tommy's nursery, and then went to work on pulling every power tool out of my garage to see if it had been used lately. They insisted it was all necessary to the investigation, but to me it all felt so senseless. Lenn and Tommy weren't at the Hollows, hadn't left a thing behind, and other than the clothes on their backs, hadn't seemed to take a thing with them.

Lenn's purse still sat on the kitchen island, keys resting right beside it.

Kel lingered in the office doorway, eyes crawling across my wife's desk before stopping. "Is that Lenn's phone?"

I spotted it on the desk, where she always left it charging. "Yeah."

"Have you looked at it?"

"Haven't touched it."

He stepped closer. "Someone should have taken that earlier for a forensics swab and then the tech department can have a look at her messages and history—"

"You think that will tell us who did this?" Anger bubbled to the surface.

Kel shrugged. "I can have the judge issue a warrant for it if you'd rather, I'm just trying to make this easy on you."

I choked on the snarl sitting in my throat.

"Get some sleep, Morrissey. Geez."

"Sleep?" I looked at him aghast, feeling a strong desire to throttle him.

He slipped Lenn's phone into an evidence bag, a flash of compassion in his eyes before it was extinguished again. "I'll give you a call in the morning and update you on anything new."

"Hopefully there is something new."

He nodded, mouth split in a thin line, before he backed out of the doorway. "I'll see myself out."

I didn't answer him, but trailed behind once I heard the front door close. I dragged my feet down the hallway, not even sure how I'd made it this long. I'd spent all the daylight hours searching the woods with the other officers today, up and down our stretch of the coast, and even into the neighbor's goat field that bordered our property. Fifty-five acres and we'd turned it upside down.

I had a feeling there would be more buzz around here tomorrow, because I knew the longer we didn't find them, the more they'd turn to me as their main suspect.

I pressed my lips together, double-checking that the security gate had closed behind Kel when he'd left, then punched in the house security system. I listened to the *beep-beeps* impassively, their ability to make me feel safe in this big sprawling estate no longer as reassuring as it once was.

My heart felt as hollow as my head. I dragged myself to the leather sectional in the living room, flipped on the fireplace, and fell into a tortured sleep.

CHAPTER SIX

Lennox
Three summers ago — July

"Lennie!" Dad's voice bellowed through the tin trailer, my feet already on the rickety front steps as I slammed the door behind me. Stuck in this little trailer with him wasn't exactly how I'd hoped to spend summer break, but he'd calmed somewhat since I'd left home for college. I think humble pie suited the old man. Still, I pretended I didn't hear him; there wasn't any other way. I'd learned that lesson the hard way over and over again.

"Your dad alright?" Morrissey raised an eyebrow. He was leaning against his Dodge Charger and looking every part the James Dean lookalike.

"He's fine. He's been drunk since noon. He just needs to pass out on the couch and sleep it off."

He half grinned, taking me in his arms and pulling me close to peck my cheek with a kiss. "You smell so good."

"Thanks." I ducked out from under him and slipped into his car. "I'm starving."

Morrissey shook his head, coming back around the car to slide behind the wheel. "What are you in the mood for?"

"Drive-in food, juicy cheeseburgers and fries and malt shakes."

"Sounds amazing." Morrissey pulled out of our tiny driveway and took off down the road. A few minutes later he was pulling into the town's vintage drive-in. It was our favorite spot, and the waitresses clamored to wait on Morrissey Monroe's car when he pulled up — his tips were outlandishly generous and he always had a smile on his face.

That was the thing about him; people, men and women, were drawn to his certain brand of humor. He had a way of making a person feel good, even when they didn't about themselves.

"Usual, kids?" Helda already had her pad out and began writing down our order.

"Two cheeseburgers, large fries and a double malt?" His warm eyes turned to me in question. I loved him then. I tried my best to not let on, but he'd had me from day one with that smile and charm that was uniquely his.

"Yes, please."

Helda left and Morrissey turned to me. "Where should we take dinner?"

I grinned, loving this part of our date. Instead of eating at restaurants, we liked to order out and find different picnic spots that only we knew. "Let's go up to the Point."

"The Point?" Surprise crossed his features. "Where we were swimming last month when Kel met that tourist girl?"

Guilt radiated through me. The last time we'd all been up here together had resulted in a tragedy that still sent shockwaves through my body. I remembered Carl's threatening words the last time I'd ran into him. It had been more than two months since the accident on the bluff, and a month had passed before I'd even seen Carl again after . . . I hadn't even realized the lasting scars that night had left. Disdain had rippled through his words then, and with so much damage already done, what would telling Morrissey and Kel change? Dwelling on the past was hopeless, so I forced myself to think only of the future.

"There's a big house up there that overlooks the lighthouse, past our old swimming spot. I want to see it."

"The Hollows? It's not that special." Morrissey shrugged. "But sure, we can take a drive that way."

"It sounds impressive. How do you think they have a house that big?"

"What?" he asked.

"You know, where do you think they work? There's not anywhere to work around here that I know of to afford a house like that."

"I don't think they work anywhere, Lenn. I think they own the vineyard and sell the wine. I'm not really sure. My dad knows the people that live there."

"Your dad?" The wheels were turning in my mind as I started to think of ways that could afford me a house like that.

Morrissey shrugged. "Yacht club members. They've got the best view of the lighthouse in Thieves Cove, that's for sure."

"I want to see it."

His grin broadened. "Then we shall see it."

He paid for our dinner when Helda dropped it off a few minutes later, sliding her an extra twenty for a tip. She winked and waved when he drove away, and I knew then that Morrissey Monroe had a way of charming people with his money. A way that I didn't have, but one day — one day maybe I would get out of this town and make something of myself.

"Fun fact," I started, "my mom and Helda were best friends in high school. She's known me since I was a baby."

"Really? The roots run deep in this town, I guess. Are they still friends?"

"They had a falling out when I was in middle school, I never found out what it was about. She used to babysit me sometimes, and when Dad came home from the bar the three of them would stay up half the night playing euchre and laughing. And her and my mom always made loaves of banana and zucchini bread and sticky cinnamon rolls that oozed with vanilla frosting when they were together, my dad's favorite. I still make him fresh cinnamon rolls every Christmas morning." I took a long sip of the icy-cold water Helda had delivered along with the double malt as memories from the past washed over me. I wondered how many years I'd have left with him, my dad's health being in shaky territory for years now. I sighed, redirecting the conversation. "You don't know good water until you haven't had running water."

"What?" He laughed.

I shrugged. "My dad and I lived on a houseboat for a while when I was little."

"For a summer or something?"

"No. For a few years."

"Years? Without running water?"

"Exactly, and that was just the tip of the iceberg. No flushing toilet, no electricity, just us and what we could gather for resources. I bathed in the bay and the day I went to kindergarten the bus picked me up at the dock. A little girl running around in sandals while the snow flies has a way of alerting people though. One of the neighbors called CPS and they gave my dad thirty days to find a permanent address. Or else."

"Or else?"

"Or else they would put me in foster care, I guess. Or track down my mom. I don't know what would be worse. Titan was a godsend when it came into town. He hired on at the warehouse and your dad gave him a paycheck advance so he had the first and last months' rent on the trailer. He loved being on the water, I think dry land ruined him a little bit. He thought I loved it — he still calls me his little water baby — but secretly, I hated it. The constant rocking made me nauseous. I never wanted to disappoint him though. I think even then I was deep down terrified someday he would leave like my mom did."

"Where was she?"

"Where *wasn't* she is a better question." I shrugged, gulping the double malt down as he drove. "She worked for a while cleaning rooms at the hotel in town but split before I was a year old. I get a birthday card with a lotto ticket every now and again, sometimes she gets the month right. She drops in on our lives once in a while to wreak havoc in person — she's good at that."

"She sounds like a peach."

"To say the least. So that's the real reason I hate water. Or the bay, specifically."

"Conquer your fears or they'll conquer you, baby."

I arched a playful eyebrow. "No thanks, I've got enough fears I'm dealing with these days."

Morrissey slowed the Charger as we took the steep bluff extra slow. Thoughts of the night Kel had the accident throbbed through my brain. I wondered if he knew the true damage he'd caused that night, if it had been an intentional coverup between him and his dad like Carl often suggested. I hated thinking about it, hated that I couldn't look Kel in the eye like I used to, hated that around every corner lurked another ghost.

Dreaming of being free of this town was about the only thing keeping me grounded these days. I only had a few short years to go and then I would have a degree and could leave the little trailer on Spruce Court and never look back. Life had taught me tough lessons, much tougher than any Morrissey had had to learn. I was sure of it, even though we were only a few months apart in age.

A few months and a thousand miles across town.

"Someday I want to leave Thieves Cove," I mused as evergreen after evergreen zoomed by my window. "But until I do, this is where I want to live."

Morrissey raised an eyebrow.

"That sounds like a great goal." He shifted the Charger into a lower gear as we began to climb a steep incline. The engine rumbled, vibrations running up and down my spine and making me feel alive with him. Before Morrissey I'd been living a life blinded by suffering, but after I had to work to contain the joy that constantly threatened my lips.

"I have to have big goals; I would die without them." I caught the twitch of his lips with my words. I winced inwardly. I'd need to keep the smell of desperation off of me if I was going to make this work. Families like the Monroes were suspicious of kids like me.

I may have left the trailer park behind when I went to college, but the stench had followed me. It had taken exactly a month for my new dorm roommate to accuse me of stealing a twenty-dollar bill.

Meanwhile, she paraded every loser she picked up after class through our room at all hours of the night. It had taken everything in me to withstand my first semester because of her alone.

"I like your big goals. My parents took me to Hawaii when I was eight. I don't remember much of it, but I remember thinking it was the most beautiful place I'd ever seen. A Garden of Eden right here on Earth. I still think of it now when I close my eyes." He paused. "I'll take you sometime. We'll go together — I have to know if it's as good as I remember."

A smile spread across my face when we crested the top of the knoll, the evergreens parting to make way for a rolling vineyard and beach, the sparkling turquoise bay dominating the view beyond. "I love this part."

He chuckled softly, slowing as we passed the dirt pull-off we normally parked at to go swimming. "Should we stop here and eat?"

"No. Take me to the lighthouse."

"Doggedly determined, are we? Okay, here we go then." He slipped the engine into a higher gear and we sped down the winding road, cherry tree branches gnarled and heavy with fat black fruit.

"That's the turn-off to your house. *The Hollows.*" He pointed.

The narrow driveway curled around a stand of cherries before stopping at a wrought-iron gate. Anchors flanked either side as twisting engraved fisherman's rope looped with an interlocking life preserver dead center.

"Spooky name for a big modern house out here by itself."

"It's named for the narrows just around the edge of the Point. Ships run aground there if the water is too low, so sailors nicknamed it the Hollows on sonar. It's the graveyard of the bay."

I tried to lift myself up on my tiptoes to get a better view from our poor vantage point. "I love it. Is that a stable too?"

"And don't forget the vineyard and bluff overlooking the lighthouse."

I could feel adrenaline pumping through my veins as I imagined the classy grandeur of an estate like that. "Can we get closer to the lighthouse?"

"Yup. Just around the corner." Just as he finished, the red-striped lighthouse came into view.

"It's breathtaking."

"It's old, and if a great view is all it takes to put a smile like that on your face—" he laced my fingers with his and brought them to his lips in a kiss — "I know my goal then. I'll take you there someday."

Warmth crept up my body, making my nerves hum to life as he pulled off onto the rocky shoulder, rolled down the windows and then cut the engine. "Closest I can get you for now."

"For now, huh?" I sunk myself close to him. "Thank you for bringing me here. It's my favorite place."

"Our favorite place."

He winked once before passing me a takeout burger. "Now eat, woman."

I laughed when he unwrapped it, taking a bite before he did. We shared the burgers that night, not because we had to but because it felt too good not to. He opened the fry bag next, uncapping the malt and swiping the fried potato through the ice cream.

"Holy disgusting habits, Batman."

"Holy you-ain't-lived-until-you've-dipped-your-fries-in-a-shake, Robin." He forced the dipped fry to my lips and I took a bite. I chewed carefully, swallowed and then smiled. "That was revolting."

He barked a laugh.

We finished eating in silence, the gentle roar of the waves only drowned out by the beats of my lovestruck heart. Soon the sun was setting, painting Castle Bay in streaks of orange and pink.

"This is my favorite place. I haven't been anywhere better than here. I'm sure there's prettier spots, but this is the prettiest I've found so far."

"I couldn't agree more." Morrissey tucked his arm around my shoulders, lips sliding against my neck and sending goosebumps in different directions. "I love being with you, Lennox McGregor. You make me laugh with the wild things that come out of your beautiful lips."

I let my eyes flutter closed, allowing the masculine scent of him to wash over me. His hands stroked the undersides of my arms, fierce volcanoes exploding in the wake of his touch. He turned my chin, catching my lips with his. His hot palm slipped from my arm to under my shirt, climbing up my cool skin and making me squirm in my chair. My breathing came out in a rush, my heart darting up into the back of my throat.

He cupped my breast, tweaking the nipple once through my cotton bra. I yelped and jumped, tears springing to my eyes as a torrent of emotion rushed through my body. I pushed his hand away, biting down on my bottom lip before formulating the most off-putting reply I could muster. "I'm not the girl for you, Morrissey Monroe. You're too experienced. I know the girls that have come before me, rumors fly around this town. I couldn't take it if they knew I gave you my virginity."

"You're a virgin?" His hands ran down my arms and landed at my wrists. He paused tenderly, his gaze cutting from mine before he backed away.

"I made a promise to myself to not give up the most sacred part of me until marriage. I know I'm hopelessly old-fashioned."

"That's not old-fashioned." He cupped my cheeks with his palms, tenderness warming his eyes. "That's positively perfect of you." He dotted my lips with a kiss. "So pure and honest. I wouldn't have you any other way."

He settled himself back in his seat, me crooked under his arm and feeling impossibly warm and fuzzy. The first sixteen years of my life felt like guerrilla warfare in comparison to moments spent with Morrissey. Peace and sweetness radiated off of him so casually, so foreign to my own experience. My hopes and dreams felt twined with his — he, my only light in an eternal dark winter.

"I should get you home before all the light is gone, your dad will have my head on one of those pylons in the bay if he suspects any foul play."

"You're not wrong about that. He protects what's his."

Morrissey shook his head. "You're in college, he could stand to ease up a little."

My eyes drifted to the house on the knoll again. "I understand why he's overprotective, I'm just lucky I have friends like you in my life to escape to."

"Friends?" Morrissey brimmed as the engine of the Charger roared to life. "We're a helluva lot more than friends."

"But he doesn't know that."

"He thinks I just take you out five nights a week for the small talk?"

"Don't you?" I cast a cocky grin at him.

His irritation broke. "I just wish we could have more time together."

"Why?" I climbed across the seat as he drove, pecking him on the cheek chastely. "So you can play with my boobs again?"

His cheeks reddened then. "I love you, Lenn. We've been together for almost a year, that's the longest I've been with anyone. You're the real deal for me, you're different from anyone I've ever met."

"I guess it's too bad you didn't find me before now."

He didn't reply, only cleared his throat and clenched his fist around the leather wheel. The big house came fully into view from this angle, my eyes wandering from his annoyed face to the two-story boathouse and wraparound dock that stretched out into the water. Spectacular ground-to-peak windows stretched across the side of the house that faced the lighthouse, a pool and outdoor kitchen and patio in the space between. It was breathtaking.

"Lenn?" I heard his voice, but I didn't *really* hear it.

"Ssh, Monroe." I pressed my finger to his lips. "I'm dreaming."

CHAPTER SEVEN

Morrissey
First night: 3.53 a.m.

"Mamamamamama."

I shot off the couch, instantly awake as I searched the room. Silence echoed loudly.

"Shit." My eyes burned as I tried to make the numbers out on the clock. Just before four in the morning. Nearly twenty-four hours ago, I was just getting up to go for that morning delivery, unaware my life was on the precipice.

Were they there before I left for work?

I wished to God I had checked.

If I had, would anything be different? I couldn't know, but it didn't stop my mind from obsessing over the range of possibilities.

"Where are you, Lenn? Talk to me," I bellowed into the hollow space. Everything she so lovingly picked to decorate our space was without life now that the two people that mattered most weren't there.

My eyes lingered on the medicine cabinet next to the built-in refrigerator. I thought of the prescription for sleeping pills the doctor had written me after too many sleepless nights of accounting had led to some unbearable bouts of anxiety. I'd nearly fallen asleep on an early morning run to Little Neck Bay, over an hour away and with only open water between here and there. Those were the kind of mistakes I couldn't afford.

I didn't have the most dangerous job, but it kept me on my toes. In truth, I kind of liked the adrenaline rush flying float planes gave me, but as I'd come to take over Dad's company, the exhaustively long hours he'd put in drained me.

The news of Tommy's impending arrival came only months later, and we were overjoyed, but in some ways the damage had already been done. Sometimes it only takes a minute to ruin a life.

When we first met, Lennox used to say she believed in ghosts and spirits and reincarnation and telepathy. I wondered if she still did. She used to say that she'd prayed so hard for the house on the hill, God had to give it to us. I liked to retort that God wasn't much help when it came to paying the mortgage, but she'd only roll her eyes.

It was cute at the time.

Before all of it was threatened in a blink.

Suddenly feeling the static energy oppressive, I flipped off the security system and opened the front door. My eyes scanned the rolling lawn that eventually tapered to the dark bay beyond. I'd grown up in these waters, I knew them better than the back of my hand, but did its murky depths hide Tommy and Lenn from me now?

I jogged a few tentative steps off the porch, the exhaustion that had rattled my bones earlier washing out to a more comfortable numbness. I sucked in sharp breaths of the autumn air, praying that wherever they were they were safe.

Maybe this had been coming and I'd been too fucking stupid to see it. Maybe she wanted freedom and suddenly the weight of our future had crashed down on both of us. Our marriage was far from perfect, but maybe I'd tricked myself into believing we were normal. Perfectly average.

"What the hell?" I froze on the spot as my eyes finally adjusted in the darkness. I hadn't wanted to take something to help me sleep in case anything happened, in case someone — *they* — showed up. But now it felt like my mind was playing nasty tricks. But it couldn't be.

A lone dark figure moving along the shore, one foot dragging slightly behind the other.

"Hey—" My voice was barely above a croak. "Hey!"

I stumbled in the direction of the boathouse, the wet rocks under my feet almost toppling me. I caught myself on the tall blades of seagrass, sliding partway down the rocks until I reached the pebbled beach. I took off at a run down to the boathouse; the figure I'd seen hunched over the dock and peering into the water a moment ago had vanished.

"Am I going insane?"

I grit my teeth, stopping at the place on the dock where I thought I'd seen the hooded figure. I was almost sure he was hooded. And tall — really tall. I fished in my pocket for my phone, cursing when I realized I'd left it up at the house. I took a few more steps into the woods, eyes searching the pine needle floor for tracks.

"I should just call."

I spun, eyes carefully searching the water where the figure had been gazing. My teeth still clamped together, I bent down further, trying to discern if shadows slipping under the water were real, or if the heavy mist rolling off the water was playing tricks with my eyes.

"I think I'm going nuts."

A cold chill spiraled down my spine and I shot up, headed back down the darkened dock and up the slippery rock pathway that led to the main house. I didn't have it in me to turn around to see if anyone was watching.

I felt it.

I felt the chill down deep in my bones.

CHAPTER EIGHT

Lennox
Three summers ago — August

"You're so bad," Morrissey sang, *"best I ever had."* The radio waves were lost to the wind as we cruised up Smokey Hollow Road, Thieves Cove in the rear-view mirror of the Charger.

"I'm going to *hate* not having you on campus this fall."

Morrissey snaked his hand between us, locking our fingers and pressing them to his lips in a quick kiss. "I'll come back for you every weekend, m'lady."

I giggled, feeling his warmth circle me like a soft blanket.

From the moment we'd met on the boat docks, I knew something was different between us. The truth of it was, I'd known Morrissey Monroe since high school, but something changed between us that last summer before I left for college.

We'd hung out in groups of friends before, but he was mister homecoming king, and I was little miss wallflower. He didn't have eyes for me then, and I wasn't interested in anything more than leaving this town in the dust. Until last summer.

Last summer with Morrissey Monroe changed everything.

While he was supposed to be going to the University of Michigan in the fall, because I was going to Central for teaching, he transferred his credits and began with me there. His dad had been furious; he was hellbent on him earning a degree at his alma mater so he could take over the family transport business someday, but Morrissey didn't want any of it. Not yet anyway.

"Hey, with any luck the old man won't retire for another decade and I'll have all the time in the world to figure it out."

I shook my head, loving the way his eyes sparkled and shone whenever he looked at me. That was the thing about being with Morrissey Monroe, it was so easy. I craved the simplicity he brought to my life.

"Do you need any help packing up your stuff?"

"No, I hardly unpacked in May. To say it's been the longest summer of my life would be an understatement."

"Well—" he pressed a kiss into my knuckles as the wind caught his unruly hair — "next summer, stay with me."

"You? Where? At your parents' house?"

Morrissey shrugged, grin widening. "Why not?"

"Well, I did spend almost every day this summer in your pool."

"See? Stay with me and save gas money. And the planet." He tacked the last bit on with a shrug.

"And your mom won't mind giving up the guest bedroom for three months?"

Morrissey nailed me with his dark eyes, and my stomach flipped. "Who said anything about the guest bedroom?"

"Me. You know the deal, Monroe, stop trying to snatch my virtue out from under me."

He winked, slowed the car and pulled into the yacht club. We passed through the valet and he waved at the attendant before his dad caught sight of the car and burst out of the gold-engraved double doors. "Morrissey!"

He stuffed a bill in the attendant's hand, slurring his son's name as he angled for the car. He stumbled once and I launched out of the front seat to help guide him the remainder of the way. He grunted when I slipped an arm under his elbow, Morrissey picking up his other arm and easing him into the front seat. "Thanks."

I buckled myself in the back, the smell of Mr. Monroe's expensive aftershave filling the cab of the car. Morrissey must have been choking on it as much as me because he cracked the window as we pulled out of the parking lot.

"How do I turn this fucking thing on?" Mr. Monroe was punching the dash screen. The drunken slur of his words didn't go unnoticed by either of us, but he was better than expected — the last time Morrissey's mom had asked him to pick his dad up at the yacht club, he'd fallen into my arms and called me his wife's name.

"Music, where's the fucking music? Too quiet in here, I can hear every single one of my thoughts." He chuckled at his own joke.

"What are you in the mood for, Dad?" Morrissey's words were smooth and monotone, emotionless. He'd done this before.

"Rolling Stones, and turn it up."

Morrissey pulled a playlist up on the screen, setting the band to play at random. The intro to "Beast of Burden" clung to us, bringing a smile to my face when Morrissey's dad began singing at the top of his range to mimic Mick Jagger. Morrissey caught my eye in the rear-view and winked, turning up the music even louder. Mr. Monroe rolled the window down, the tie that was fastened at his neck whipping in the wind like a noose.

Happiness. Always sweet and ever fleeting.

CHAPTER NINE

Morrissey
Second day: 6.22 a.m.

"Morrissey!" I heard Kel's voice before I saw him. I crested the hill, his police cruiser finally coming into view, his tiny frame sunk inside the shadows. "Tried knocking on the door, but you left it open. You make a habit of that?"

"Of what?" I growled when I was close.

"Leavin' the door wide open. How long have you been out, Morrissey?"

I reached the front door, flipping on the lights. "Good morning to you too."

"Morrissey." Kel's usual subtle limp was more pronounced.

"You always provide this level of in-person service for your other jobs?"

"For my other missing persons cases — yeah, Morrissey, as a matter of fact I do." Kel shoved at my bicep just like he used to when we were kids. "When I'm wearing this badge, our history means shit to me. I'm here to bring your family home, that's all. Don't insult me for doing my job."

"Well, maybe you're barking up the wrong tree on this." I slammed my hand against the marble counter.

"And whose tree do you think I'm barking up, Morrissey? Why don't you tell me? I know this is hard on you, but while you're out there wandering the beach, doing God knows what, I'm knee-deep in shit searching for your little boy. Now, why do you think I came here so goddamn early?" Kel tossed a manilla folder on the counter. "We need to talk about what exactly you saw when you left yesterday morning."

"I told you." I sank onto the stool, defeat softening my muscles. "Nothing. I woke up to my alarm, got dressed in the dark. I didn't stop to check if Lenn was in bed beside me or in the office, I just . . . assumed she was."

"You didn't stop to give her a kiss or leave a note or tell her when you'd be back or—?"

"No, no, I didn't do any of that." The words felt callous even to myself. We'd stopped saying 'I love you' around the time Tommy was born. Goodbye kisses had fizzled out along with it, I guess.

"Well, she was here, Morrissey. At least, that's what the footage shows. You sure you don't have cameras set up anywhere else, in the foyer or around the kitchen?" His eyes shot around the recessed crown-molded ceilings.

"Security inside?" I shook my head. "I didn't think we needed it."

"You'd be surprised how many domestic disputes would go the other way if couples had cameras turned indoors."

I grit my teeth. "What are you getting at, Kel?"

Kel only sighed. "The security cameras caught something. I can't make it out, it's way out the back of your property, but the night in question, it appears someone was out back burying something in your vineyard."

"What?" Terror flooded my system. "Well, who was it?"

"It's hard to make out, I was hoping you could recognize the frame at least." He indicated the folder.

I smacked my palm down on it, sliding it my way and opening it. Copy after copy of grainy surveillance photos. A stack of two dozen at least, and the only ones that were relevant to me were the ones time-stamped with her car coming home after eleven at night, and mine pulling out of our front gates at 4.44 a.m. the following morning for work.

"I don't see anything."

Kel pulled a tiny magnifying glass from his jacket pocket and held it above one of the grainiest images. "See there?"

I squinted. Squinted harder. Swiped my glasses off the counter and squinted again. "It looks like a ghost."

Kel huffed, moving the magnifier to another photo. "I was hoping you could tell by the size of the frame though; it looks like they could be wearing a hood—"

"It looks like a fucking shadow, Kel. You drove all the way out here at quarter to six in the morning to show me a fucking boogeyman?" I sent the photos flying off the counter. Exasperation and exhaustion were fighting a war inside my head.

"Morrissey, we've got to follow procedure on this."

"Fuck your procedures, did you call the Feds in on this, Kel?"

Kel pressed his lips closed and I knew I had him. Federal agents were his soft spot. For as long as I'd known him, Kel and his sheriff father had nothing but unkind things to say about federal cases and the shitshow job the agents always did. "I don't think we need their help on this, Morrissey, not yet. But I promise you, it doesn't matter what I feel personally, I wouldn't risk the life of your son and wife if I thought they could help us here."

Bile rose in my throat. "I hope that's true."

"Well, I know you're not gonna like this next part, but I figured the least you and I can do is take a walk and go investigate that part of the property, search for a clue or some evidence of someone digging recently."

"There's nothing out there but the grape crusher."

"The grape crusher?" Kel repeated. "My guys didn't mention that in the report. Did one of us search that corner of the vineyard yesterday?"

"How would I know? I was all over the place, I can't keep track of what your guys searched or not yesterday, that's why I was out hunting around tonight, I couldn't sleep, and I . . . I just . . ." I gulped, ragged thoughts finally turning disjointed.

"I got it, buddy." Kel clapped me on the shoulder. "Let's take a walk and we can talk about it."

On heavy feet, I dragged my ass across the kitchen and out the front doors again, this time the early dawn light cascading across the vineyard and highlighting our lost harvest.

"Lenn was telling me a few weeks ago when I ran into her at the gas station that the grape harvest went tits up this year. I'm sorry to hear that — one vintner across the bay said that the frost we got early this spring took out half of his crop."

"We didn't have half a crop to take out. Neighbor's goats slip through the fence weekly and have a feast. Our crop was devoured before we had a chance to get fruit."

"Lenn said she tried to talk to him, but every time she goes down to his house there's no answer. I told her if it continued to be a problem, I'd be happy to make a house call."

"I'm sure you would." This probably wasn't the time for sarcasm, but what was it the time for?

"Maybe you can hunt down a goat-resistant grape."

I wondered if he was being serious or not. It reminded me why Lenn always seemed to carry a torch of disdain for Kel — we'd grown apart over the last few years, but Lenn especially seemed to bristle when I mentioned talking to Kel now and again. "You want me to replant fifty acres of grapes and scrap the heritage crop the Hollows is known for?"

Kel shrugged, eyes turning to the field in front of us. We walked beneath the tall rows, brown leaves dripping from trellises where plump fruit should be. "Hell, that's your grape press?" The shock winding through his eyes was evident. "Lenn told me she was going to use some ancient barrel press powered by the bay to crush the grapes; this is industrial-sized."

"Lenn had big dreams of turning this place into the best boutique vineyard the coast's ever seen. I don't think she accounted much for the learning curve."

"The folks that were here before you were third-generation winemakers."

"I know, I know, but they didn't leave us the instruction manual. You'd think financing two and a half million would get you a guidebook or two, but the only thing we know about winemaking is what Lenn researched online."

"They sure bailed out of here fast."

I shrugged as we turned the corner of the wine barn. "Don't know why, don't care. Only wish I knew a guy lookin' for an industrial wine press. I called the company that makes it, but turns out it was shipped here from Germany, and there's no return policy. Selling that monster would help offset the loss of the grapes, but I can't find anyone that needs one."

"The long winters lately have shut down a lot of the vineyards." Kel stepped closer to the grape crusher, taking his hat off as he stuck his head inside the feed chute. "This is a monster."

I nodded.

"You ever cleaned these blades?"

I stuck my head in the chute once he'd finished, surprised to find more than two dozen sharpened steel blades sticking up at the bottom of a basin and platform, remembering when Lenn had warned that once the engine gathered momentum, the spinning blades could take up to a minute to slow back down again.

"Honestly? We've never used the thing. Lenn was in a tizzy once Tommy started crawling — he loves big machines and his eyes always grow big when we walk around this side of the field. She stopped letting him come this way altogether because he'd try to climb up anywhere he could, so they started walking down by the beach . . ."

I trailed off, wondering if that small decision had been a deciding factor in their fate.

Kel's eyes lingered long and hard on me. An uneasy feeling bloomed low in my stomach. Why hadn't I thought to come check the giant piece of machinery that anchored one corner of our property? I guess because the possibility was too horrific for even my mind to imagine.

"If I check the security footage, I won't find this in use over the last few days, right?"

"Kel, what are you saying? You think I'm lying?"

Kel frowned, eyes still nailed on mine. I swallowed, feeling every barb of suspicion he threw my way. I knew what procedure taught him to look for, I knew I was the prime suspect, but just because probability wasn't on my side didn't make it fact.

"If you don't believe me, get your guys out here then." I waved him off, stomping back down the grape row.

"Morrissey—" he jogged to catch up — "you know I have to explore all options."

I didn't reply, only quickened my pace. I couldn't handle his scrutiny, not now, maybe not ever.

"Morrissey — I think it's time we held a press conference."

I turned my eyes on him, mouth dropping open as I thought what that might mean.

"Give you a chance to appeal to whoever took them, or ask if anyone saw anything suspicious last night."

I shook my head. "What am I supposed to say?"

"Whatever is in your heart, Morrissey. People just want to hear what's in your heart."

My shock was interrupted by a soft drawl. "We were wonderin' where we'd find you two. I just wanted to drop off a breakfast casserole for Morrissey."

Macy Thurston, the realtor that had sold us the Hollows, thrust out a dish.

Kel didn't respond, only looked at me.

"Thanks." I didn't bother taking it, only kept walking to my front door, hearing the call of my couch and a pillow. Maybe I would take a sleeping pill, maybe if Kel and his crew were going to be around again searching the property today I could just knock myself out and get a few hours of restless sleep.

"I just wanted to stop by and offer up my services. Most people don't like to stay in a place with bad juju. I can get this on the market for ya by end of closing today, and with the high-end client list I have at my fingertips we could probably get the Hollows off of your hands by weekend."

I glanced at Macy as she followed me into the house, Kel fast behind her.

"That wife of yours has an eye for real estate, sending me links to different properties all the time."

"Really?" I frowned, then caught myself.

One more secret Lenn had kept, a penchant for high-end real estate.

"Spalding can stop over anytime too," she continued after me. "He's eighteen now and got an apartment of his own, and he's strong as a horse — if you need any help around the vineyard, he'd be here in two shakes. He's always looking for odd jobs and farm work."

"We lost the grapes to goats this season. Unless Spalding knows how to fly a Cessna . . ."

"You need someone to make your runs while you're focused on this?" Kel stepped forward. "My brother-in-law spent some time delivering fuel in the Arctic Circle. He's been back a few years now, I can give him a call and see if he wants to take a few of your deliveries."

Annoyance lit in me.

"What I really want is a nap." I slouched down on the sofa, eyes casting off to the cloudy bay. "And I want you to find them, Kel. I want you to work a helluva lot harder than you've been, and I want you to bring my family home."

"I'll get a press conference together then, does later this afternoon work for you?"

"Whatever you say, Kel. Oh, and . . ." I thought of the hooded shadow I'd seen down by the bay, and how it looked like nothing more than a ghost the more I thought about it.

"And?" he pressed.

"And nothing. See you later, Kel."

I didn't see him leave, only heard the door close on his way out.

"You want me to lock up the security system now that Officer Kendry is gone?" Macy moved closer, patting me on the shoulder.

I stared at the floor, at a loss for words for all of this.

Had it been a shadow I'd seen? Or maybe a neighbor? I hadn't thought of asking, because I'd only assumed Kel's officers had, but how did they know to ask the right questions?

And what were the right questions? Our nearest neighbor was the goat farmer, the closest after that clear across the bay. We owned all of the Point outside of the tiny ten-acre parcel that butted the south corner of our property.

"Lost in thought? I'll leave you, I'm sure I'm just takin' up all of your time."

"Thank you for thinking of me, Macy." I lay back on the couch, pulling a throw pillow over my head.

"Sure, Morrissey. You know, ever since I heard you and Lenn got married after all of these years . . . We just went through so much together . . . Well, I don't know what's going on around this town, but I'm here for you. I always have been, and always will be. No matter how this turns out, you can count on me."

Her hand was on my shoulder again, the thick chemicals in her dollar store perfume making me cough. "Thanks, Macy, I know Lennox would appreciate it too."

She cleared her throat. I sensed her shuffle. "Call me if you need anything, Morrissey. I'll stop by later this week for my casserole dish."

I groaned before I heard the door close.

That was the thing about growing up in a small town, before you knew it your middle school crush has turned into an unbearable, sickly-sweet caricature of adulthood. Living out on the Point may have cost us everything, but at least it afforded us the privacy from people that lacked any self-awareness.

Aside from our run-ins with the goat farmer, we'd had it pretty good out here. Sandwiched between the lighthouse and the vineyard, we'd found our bliss. And then life took an ice pick to it, chipping away at us one twisted moment at a time.

Desperate for a change of scenery, I jumped off the couch and strode down the hallway, intent on a hot shower. I was pulling my shirt over my head when I passed Lenn's office and a blinking red dot caught my eye.

I ducked in, drawn to her office desk and the phone that sat on top of it. Lenn and I always kept our business lives separate; I would never answer one of her work calls about the vineyard or charter school charity events, but now . . . now I had a motive.

I winced at my inner choice of words before hitting play on the voicemail. "Hi Lenn, Waller and Associates here. I just wanted to follow up with you on the property rights violation we talked about filing. I've looked into some property law cases and, like I said, I think we can threaten to sue until he cleans up his act on this situation. Anyway, give me a call back and I can get moving on the paperwork."

The message went silent.

I gulped.

Property law? I didn't think, only hit redial on the last call and waited as it rang. Finally, a machine picked up and I left a message. "Hello, this is Lennox Monroe's husband. She's . . ." I struggled to find the words. "She's not here right now, I just wanted to know what you were working with her on." I cringed as I realized how truly awful my words sounded. "You know how to get a hold of me. Thanks."

I slammed the handset back into the base and stalked to the bathroom, mind suddenly abuzz with what exactly that call meant. Lenn was smart — whatever she was doing, I was sure there was a logical reason for it. We just hadn't had a chance to talk about it yet.

I turned the water to scalding hot, thankful when the tiny needles sliced into my skin and left stinging red marks. I needed to feel something. I'd been a walking zombie since yesterday morning. My thoughts had turned and twisted on me, the lack of sleep causing hallucinations or delusions. At this rate I would be no good in a cockpit even if I could haul myself to the hangar.

I splashed my face, willing my sweet boy and wife home for the millionth time. I'd already thought about hiring a private investigator, but at this point, what good was that when I was already financed to the hilt with the business and the house — what could the investigator turn up that I couldn't anyway? I would just need to focus more — make finding them my full-time job and not keeping my father's transport business afloat all of these years later.

Sharp basslines sliced through the steamy air then, the sound system in the house suddenly on full blast as the chorus of an old Steve Miller song echoed around me. "What in the world?"

I cut the water and wrapped my waist with a towel, the persistent beats pounding through my skull. I snatched up my phone, wondering if it was connected to the stereo and I'd bumped the playlist by mistake — but unless there was a time delay on my stereo, that didn't make sense. I wandered out of the bedroom and into the office next door where we kept the sound system. All the lights were on, the mode set to Bluetooth.

I growled, realizing I still hadn't found the source of the music. I turned off the system and it died quickly. I waited, looking around the room to locate a potential source for the signal when all the lights flashed back on and the same song started. "The Joker" thundered out as loudly as the stereo would play, the entire house vibrating like a college frat party.

I yanked the chord from the wall and the noise died. "There, fucker."

I hated that song. Hated it with a deadly passion. I clamped my eyes shut, the vibrant rock riffs still ringing in my head, a soundtrack to death. I blinked back the memories, leaving the office and slamming the door as I went.

The last time I heard that song on repeat, I'd walked in to find my father hanging from a beam, pool hose wrapped around his neck in a makeshift noose. His body swayed and I vomited as Steve Miller jammed up my ear canals.

My heart hammered as I thought again about calling Kel. He'd think I was fucking nuts if I did, no one could possibly know that story. I'd never told a soul, not even Lennox, about my visceral reaction to that song. Was it possible my mind was somehow playing tricks on me? Had I thumb-slipped on a song from a band that I've refused to listen to for almost two years?

I went back to the bedroom, flopping down on our king-size bed and using the remote to bring the smart TV to life. I needed a distraction. I was desperate for it. I selected the family photo tab and smiled as pictures of Tommy's birth five months ago popped up on the screen. His chubby cheeks brought tears to my eyes. I wondered if the last time I'd set him in his crib would be the last time I'd hold him. I flicked further back in time to the year before that, when Lenn and I got married.

Just the two of us, right here on the Point. We started our forever here, had it ended here too?

I gulped, the pain as real and physical as a bullet.

I couldn't imagine selling this house. But without them, I couldn't imagine staying either.

I turned up the volume when a video of our first dance began to play. Our reception was humble, less than twenty of our closest friends and family, but one of the happiest days of my life. When Lenn finally let me put a ring on her finger, I'd about lost my mind with the sheer happiness of it.

I smiled, feeling wetness on my cheeks as the videographer zoomed in on our faces while we danced. An acoustic version of "Every Breath You Take" by Sting played in the background as we soaked up all the happiness. In the puffy princess dress she'd dreamed of, and me in white linen, we'd exchanged vows on our beach without knowing that the worst was just around the bend for us.

CHAPTER TEN

Lennox
Two summers ago — early June

"Morrissey!" I screamed, flying through the grand entrance of his parents' house, headed straight for the pool.

"What's up?" He must have heard my scream. He caught me just as I came over the landing and onto the patio tile.

"My dad," I blurted, heart hammering. "He was laid off today. Did your dad say anything?"

Morrissey scrunched his eyes closed. "No, I haven't seen him in a few days. Mom had a meeting in Detroit and won't be home 'til late. She texted that Dad was at the yacht club and might need a ride home."

"He hasn't said anything about Titan Transport going under?"

"Going under? Why would the business go under? He has more contracts than he can handle."

"But Dad said your dad isn't paying the bills. Workers are cashing paychecks on Friday and they're bouncing. And the pensions — they're gone."

"What are you talking about? That can't be true, that's supposed to be my business someday."

I heaved a breath, steeling my spine for the new territory both of us were in. "Everyone was laid off today, Dad came home early. They let go of everyone but Travis, who makes the island deliveries, and the flight mechanic."

"Layoffs? I'm pretty sure he would mention upcoming layoffs."

"Unless they weren't planned. It's the first Monday of the month, Morrissey, everyone got their paychecks this weekend but no one got paid."

"That's more than three hundred people, warehouses and eighteen-wheelers and—"

"Everything. Dad's already into his second pint. I had to get out of there. I couldn't listen to him cuss and berate your dad anymore."

"Shit, maybe I should go get him at the club. My dad isn't going to be in any shape to get home."

I thought of another time Morrissey had covered a drunk's tracks, and how that particular night Kel's irresponsibility had nearly cost a life on the bluff. In effect it had. I understood why Morrissey didn't want his father behind the wheel of a car, but I also hated that the man I loved seemed to attract the sort of people that needed saving.

"Maybe let him decompress, he probably doesn't want to face anyone right now."

Morrissey frowned, his eyes glazing with tenderness before he pulled me into his arms and pressed a kiss to my forehead. "I love you so much, if I haven't said it lately."

"I love you back." I inhaled him deeply, thankful for the warmth of him radiating into me and soothing away all of my worries.

"Do you need help with anything? Is there enough food at the house? Or, Lenn, please, the offer still stands — stay here. You can have the pool house to yourself. No hanky-panky, I swear." Morrissey's crooked grin lit my heart on fire. He had me so wrapped up in him that maybe, just maybe, I would violate my vow to save myself for marriage for him. But that's why I loved Morrissey so much: he never pressured me to do anything I wasn't ready for.

"As tempting as it would be to shack up here with you all summer, I'm okay at home. For now."

Morrissey's parents, despite all their failings, had raised him to think the best of people and seek kindness over judgment. He was just the kind of guy that was looking for a fledgling bird to save.

He laced our fingers and walked to the edge of the pool. He dropped down, dipping his legs in and patting the tile at his side. "Join me, pretty lady."

I giggled, thankful for the tiny respite from the hellish chaos that waited at home with Dad. He was worried about paying the bills, not that they were much. My college tuition billed more than his annual income, but thankfully I had a college fund set up from the time I was a baby. The interest had compounded so much on it as I'd grown up, it more than covered what I could spend on tuition, and I'd already placed a call to my trustee about withdrawing some of the principal early.

It would take me a few days, but I wouldn't let Dad go under. We'd been through so much, despite all the vicious arguments we'd had through all of my teen years and beyond. He'd been there for me, and I would always be there for him. Now, I would prove it.

My phone chose that moment to buzz in my back pocket. I slipped it out of my cutoffs, surprised to find a text message from my dad. His tiny flip phone was ancient, so the fact that he'd managed to type out a message was impressive to say the least.

Your mom is here.

My heart jumped into my throat. "Oh shit."

"Another *oh shit* moment? I can't handle any more today."

"My mom is back." My eyes crawled up to meet his.

"Your mom?" Morrissey frowned.

"Who knows where she was this time."

I thought of the last time she'd shown up unexpectedly and the weeks of fighting that ensued between my parents. Under the best of circumstances, they were a challenge, together a total nightmare. "God, I hope she doesn't stay long. She came back the summer I turned sixteen and I wished she hadn't. I may take you up on that bed for the summer after all."

"That bad, huh?"

"That bad," I confirmed. "She left for the first time when I was a baby, and it's probably the best gift she could have given me."

Morrissey caught me in his arms, hauling me against him and pushing his tongue past my lips in a sensual kiss. We soaked up the sun just like that, our hands exploring skin, our lips tasting each other, and barely hanging onto the last threads of control I knew we both had. "What's mine is yours, anytime. I don't care how crazy you are."

"Crazy doesn't begin to cover it." I giggled.

We'd been dating for almost three years, and so much of it was apart. The start of this summer was the first we'd seen each other in more than three months after exams and essays dominated most of our spring schedules. Morrissey had transferred to the University of Michigan to complete his business degree, just like he'd promised his dad, but I wondered if that would change now that the family business might not be there for him when he graduated.

By the time the sun was setting over the pool, Morrissey's hand was up my shirt, his lips connecting with my nipple beneath the thin fabric. "Morrissey—"

I pushed him back easily, pressing my swollen lips together. "We should . . . chill."

"Right." He smiled, a beautiful, reckless grin. "How about we order pizza?"

"That sounds . . . perfect."

CHAPTER ELEVEN

Morrissey
Second day: 1.23 p.m.

"What was the last thing you said to your wife?"

"Excuse me?"

Kel pushed me aside. "Please, please, let's stay focused."

"Mr. Monroe, you want us to believe you have no idea where Lennox and Tommy are?"

The way the reporter used their names, with a snarl on her lips, like it was meant to hurt me, made me flush with anger. I closed my eyes, palms prickling with sweat at my side.

"Okay, you lot are about as helpful as always." Kel waved them off. "Why don't you print that in your damn papers?"

A dozen voices spoke at the same time in protest.

He held up a hand, threatening to walk away before one clear voice rang out. "Officer Kendry, do you think this is a repeat of the Water Baby case?"

My ears buzzed as a reporter thrust a microphone in Kel's face. There was a small crowd gathered around our house gate. Some faces I'd seen before, but many were new. Most seemed to know exactly what this reporter was talking about though.

I narrowed my eyes, anxious for Kel's answer.

"Too early to say. Thank you for your time." He rambled off the tip line number one last time before waving at the group and stepping away from the microphones.

"What was that about?" I asked when he was near enough.

"What?" He shoved a hand in his pocket.

"The Water Baby case, what is that?"

Kel's eyes shot up. "You really don't know?"

I shook my head.

"Oh, I forgot, your family didn't move here until we were in middle school." He leaned back on his cruiser. "Still, I woulda thought Lenn would have said something over the years."

I waited, eyes holding his, anxious for more details.

"When Lenn was little, her ma and pa used to live on a houseboat not far off the marina. They fought so bad most nights, people across the bay could hear their shouting matches. No one paid any mind to them, until one night when that little baby girl of theirs went missing."

"What?" Disbelief rattled through me.

Kel shrugged. "She didn't tell you any of this?"

"Not a word," I breathed.

"Nobody could find her for two full days. The *Thieves Cove Gazette* headline read: *WATER BABY VANISHED*. My grandma held onto the newspaper, it was so striking with the bay and lighthouse taking up the front-page spread. She saved it the day they found baby Lenn too. It read: *WATER BABY FOUND*.

"There wasn't any explanation of the circumstances, only stating that the baby was found safe under suspicious circumstances and the investigation was ongoing. So many people were touched by the story, it made national headlines and a fund was set up. I think Lenn got enough money to get through college; that's what the news reported anyway.

"My grandma loves a good mystery, so she played private investigator for years trying to track down the abductor. She never found anything. Didn't stop her from calling the tip line though, even after baby Lenn was found; grandma was convinced there was a child trafficking ring operating in the area."

"Really? Wait — that's why her dad calls her his water baby. I thought it was so innocent because they lived on a houseboat for a while, but . . . I-I don't understand why she didn't tell me."

"Morrissey." His hand was at my shoulder. "I'm doin' what I can."

"I know, but I'm going insane out here. Have you interviewed the neighbors and asked if they saw anything? It just doesn't make sense that she would be out by the shore at night, not by her own choice, Kel. My wife and I have had our issues, but trust me on that. I know her more than myself on this. She hates the water, hates the bay."

"You sure about that?" Kel looked at me askance, then his eyes landed on something over my shoulder. I turned just in time to find one long, lean stilettoed heel stepping out onto the stone driveway.

"Hello?" I met her as she crossed the distance.

"Morrissey? It's Fawn Fitzgerald — I'm an attorney now. You called my office earlier about your wife?"

My throat cracked.

Fawn and I went way back.

I heard Kel huff from behind me. "Lot of good lawyering up does, Morrissey. Wish you would have told me before you went and hired this viper."

Fawn lifted her smartphone to her lips and smiled as she spoke into the microphone: "Law enforcement: *unhelpful.*"

Kel raised an eyebrow before ducking behind the wheel of his patrol car and firing it up.

As he backed out, he left a small remaining group of reporters in his wake, all of them now aiming their lenses at the two of us.

"Shit." The two of us here together, *alone*, didn't look good at all.

"So, Morrissey—" she slung her briefcase strap over one shoulder — "shall we go inside?"

CHAPTER TWELVE

Morrissey
Second day: 1.54 p.m.

Fawn's eyes swept the room, appreciating all the time Lenn had put into every element of the decor. "If I would have known things would turn out this way, maybe I wouldn't have been so quick to break up with you our sophomore summer."

I cringed when she referenced our long, long forgotten past. I said my next words under my breath. "I've been devastated ever since."

I think she caught them, sensing my sarcasm before she tipped her chin and smirked. "Your wife had big plans for this place, Mr. Monroe. But I'm sure you know that."

"How long have you been working with my wife exactly?"

"Not long." Her gaze swept back to mine. "If you would have told me you were in trouble, Morrissey—" Fawn moved closer — "I could have figured something out. You know your dad and Titan Transport were the biggest accounts at my firm."

Were.

"Well, I'm not in need of a lawyer, and you still haven't told me why exactly you and my wife had business together."

She pressed her lips together. "Well, I shouldn't really tell you this. Attorney–client privilege still applies even when it's mundane, you know. But your wife reported some troubles with the neighbor next door. Something about a lost wine crop and a second mortgage."

I winced. She knew more than I'd anticipated. "And?"

"Well, your limited insurance plan doesn't cover loss of harvest under any circumstances. Something I would advise you consider. One bad season with a late arctic clipper and your crop is wiped out before it's even started to produce for you."

"You don't say?" I deadpanned. "How much is your hourly rate again? I'm afraid I didn't catch that — or, wait, you didn't offer it, did you? Am I to assume this advice is free then?"

"Morrissey—" she stepped closer, hand on my shoulder — "considering the circumstances and our shared history, I hope you know I would do anything to help put you and your family back together again."

I bristled.

"Lenn mentioned some other options . . . She told me to find any means necessary to get your neighbor off of his property — she was willing to buy it from him — at *any* cost."

"That doesn't make sense, you said yourself we're mortgaged to the hilt, there isn't any wiggle room for down payments to expand the land. Plus, that old farmer has lived there since we were kids. Lenn wouldn't just drive him off his property. I know we've had our issues, but she would have told me if . . ."

Fawn frowned. "She seemed pretty upset about it, Morrissey. She was out for blood. She showed me the projections of the first year of wine production if all would have gone off without a hitch, and it would have been enough to pay the mortgage off on this place *and* your parents'. In *one* season."

"I can't believe this." I pushed a hand through my hair. She sat at my side, one hand rubbing my back as she pushed off her heels and flattened her pencil skirt. "I told her not to depend on the harvest to pay the bills, but the moment we got into this place it's gone one way for us."

"Nobody accused the wine business of being *good* business."

I huffed at her comment, instantly regretting that I'd even let this woman into the house. "Well, thanks for the house call, I don't want to waste your time. Lenn should have been up front with you — we just can't afford to keep a lawyer. I haven't even been paying myself. I've sold two float planes and a barge just to make payroll this year, so the business is taking everything out of us right now."

She slipped her shoes back on her feet and stood, eyes warming as she hovered at my side. "I'm sorry I bothered you, your wife just seemed so distraught the last time we chatted . . . If you know her like you say you do, then . . . well, was she on any medications? She seemed erratic to me; it sounds like we're talking about two totally different people." Her eyes landed on the highchair where Tommy normally sat eating his Cheerios. "Forgive me for saying so, but too much isolation can go to a woman's head."

I let her words hang between us, thinking how much that ship had already sailed.

"I'll leave the paperwork for you. Good luck finding your wife, and if the day comes you can't afford to *not* have a lawyer, I'm your woman. Okay, Monroe?"

I nodded, wishing this day had never happened. Or the last string of them. I led her to the front door and she stepped outside.

"Oh." Fawn bent to pick up a bright-green sticky note. "Hidden behind the mums—" she flicked the note my way — "maybe it's a clue."

I grunted, flipping the note over to find three words in dark black scratch: *Monroe killed me.*

"Is this a joke?" My eyes shifted over her shoulder, certain I'd find a punky junior reporter slinking away.

Nothing.

"Did you do this?" I fumed.

"Me?" Her eyebrows squished together. "Of course not, what is it?"

She took the note from my hands before I could stuff it in my pocket. "Oh."

"It's bullshit," I uttered, the only thing I could think to say.

"Maybe." She pressed her lips together. "You ready to rethink that lawyer now?"

I shook my head, headache burning up the base of my skull. "Fine."

"We're going to have to hand this over to Officer Kendry." She pulled her phone from her bag and held the note at arm's length before snapping a photo. "I'll send this to you."

"No." I backed into the house, no longer feeling safe with the door hanging wide open. I mentally went through the list of windows and doors throughout the house, thinking I should check them before I went to sleep tonight. And maybe make sure I had a handful of bullets next to my pistol in the nightstand.

"Morrissey." She stepped in after me. "I'll represent you — free of charge, of course — just because we go way back and you must be going through the worst thing anyone could right now, but you have to be upfront with me."

I stumbled back into a barstool, feet swept out from under me as I sat in a rush.

"Was your wife on any medication?"

"I-I don't really know. I don't think so, she didn't mention any, but you don't really . . ." I hated the words. Hated them just for swirling into my thoughts. "You don't think she did this, do you?"

"It doesn't matter what I think, Morrissey."

She straightened her spine before rifling a hand in her bag and pulling out a handful of pages. She pulled a manila envelope out, thrusting it at me. "You need to sign these before we go any further."

"Did you make Lenn sign the same attorney–client privacy stuff?" I grumbled.

"Of course, she was my client. Separate from you."

"Was?"

"*Is*," she corrected.

I signed and initialed the paperwork, making Fawn my official lawyer. I didn't know what I was doing, but I knew I was in over my head and I needed someone else on my team to help me think clearly.

"There it is then. My next question," her eyes locked onto mine, "are *you* on any medications?"

I stared blankly back at her, thinking how the second she left I would be headed to my prescription of sleeping pills.

Tonight of all nights.

"None."

CHAPTER THIRTEEN

Lennox
Two summers ago — early June

The opening guitar licks of "Beast of Burden" echoed through the pool house, pulsing through the surround sound speakers into the guest bedroom. I fumbled for my phone in search of a clock, wondering what Morrissey might be up to now.

"Mm, I've missed you, baby." One roughened palm pushed under my shirt and grasped at my breast. "You can't keep me away anymore."

"No." I could barely utter the word, so sure this was a dream and I was frozen to the spot with muscle paralysis. The hand squeezed the flesh of my breast again, pinching tenderly before hot lips connected at my neck. He sucked hard, the familiar scent of aftershave stinging my nostrils as I cried.

Another hand slipped between my thighs and fumbled as Mick Jagger screamed "never, never" through the sound system.

"No." My hands shook, cold fear drenching my skin. Was my voice even working? "*No-no-no.*"

But the song played on, surging through my ears, pulsing like a real live monster as he pushed the leg of my shorts aside and slipped inside of me.

"I've fucked up, baby, I've done bad things. I've ruined lives. It's killing me not telling you, but it'd kill you more if I did."

I cried. I cried so hard and slammed my eyes closed and dug my fingernails into the flesh of his biceps. They were familiar. Too familiar. My tears ran harder.

"I don't tell you you're pretty often enough. I loved you so much, I wanted to be good for you, tried to make you proud, but it's just not in me anymore." His rough kiss at my lips left violent tingles. "Remember when we used to go out on the boat and do little white lines in the sunshine and listen to the Stones? I just want to feel free like that again."

"Please." I gripped at the sheets, Mick Jagger screaming as the drum beat vibrated through my heart and mimicked the fast jerking movements of the man inside of me. I fisted my palms in the sheets, trying to tear away from the heavy weight of his dominant body.

"I never meant to do any harm, I didn't. I know it won't seem that way, but believe me, baby . . ." Liquor seeped out of his veins and into mine, filling the air with the stench of desperation with every slow thrust and pump. "We don't make love anymore. I hate feeling so far away from you."

"Please. Please, stop," I begged as the chorus of the song drowned me out. Finally, the thrusting turned erratic before jerking to a halt.

Sweet stillness.

Hot tears shredded my cheeks in the darkness before the heavy weight lifted, and just like a ghost, evaporated as quickly as he'd come. Hot liquid soaked my thighs and the sheets beneath me.

It couldn't be true.

It couldn't be true.

My core throbbed, evidence that every vicious second of it had been.

My fingers shaking, I pushed myself off of the bed, wishing to God I would have thought to lock the door — wishing to God I'd stayed home tonight, whether Mom was there and fighting with Dad or not. Anything would have been better than this.

My muscles trembled. The desire to take a shower and scrub the feel of him off of me was strong.

But the need to run was stronger.

I pushed my sneakers on my feet, shoving my arms in my Central hoodie before barging down the hallway. I prayed that the man that had just violated me was gone, but staying a second longer in this place was no longer an option.

The door that opened to the pool hung wide open, my stomach churning because I knew I hadn't left it that way.

I shivered, feeling like a stranger in a lost land as I ran around the edge of the pool and out of the gate. Fishing for my keys in my pocket, I didn't bother to hook my seat belt before reversing out of Morrissey Monroe's driveway faster than I ever had.

Just like that, my virtue had vanished.

CHAPTER FOURTEEN

Morrissey
Third day: 9.09 a.m.

"Kel—" I cleared my throat — "I . . . ugh, found a thing. A letter." I frowned at my reflection. "Officer Kendry, there's a note."

I pushed a hand over my head, evidence of my restless night all over my face. I'd been too afraid to take two sleeping pills like the prescription suggested and compromised on one.

Just in case . . . *anything*.

Now I wished I had taken two or three.

Every time I'd closed my eyes last night, just when my mind would drift off, I'd wake up to the opening lines of "The Joker." And the more exhausted I grew, the more my mind played tricks, twisting the lyrics of the song to fit my father's unexplained suicide.

He hadn't left a note, hadn't left anything — only left me to find him hanging, that horrible song playing over and over. Mom was already on her way home from Detroit by the time I called her that morning, and Kel and his dad were the reporting officers when I called in the emergency.

Another day I would give anything to scrub from my mind.

I thought of Lenn's warm arms around me, the way she'd brought me back to life when everything else felt hollow. I'd owed her everything then, which is why I'd proposed so quickly. Days after we'd buried my father, I asked her to marry me on the Point. It was beautiful, but nowhere near as beautiful as the smile on her face when she said yes.

And now I had to call Kel and report another emergency . . . that I'd found a note, a note that implicated me in the death of . . . *someone.*

My heart cracked behind my chest plate as I imagined what it meant — that my wife was dead. My boy, gone forever. I hadn't had it in me to call Kel and report the note. I'd nearly dropped into my bed with exhaustion, but then found the raging peace and quiet too oppressive.

Which is why I then found myself in front of the bathroom mirror, practicing how I'd break it to my childhood friend that apparently, in fact, according to this stupid green sticky note, I was the killer he was looking for.

I gave up, realizing there was no good way to sound innocent when all signs pointed one way.

I stumbled out of the bathroom, aiming for the kitchen and a giant glass of water before I hit the pillow. Coming around the corner, my eyes scanned the dark kitchen, and a flash on the closed-circuit screen in the corner drew me in.

A room.

A bed.

A baby.

"Tommy?"

The grainy screen flickered to black. I scanned the other tiny screens, searching the video feeds as I confirmed the side yard, the gates, and the driveway were all as normal.

But what was that image?

Was it really Tommy? Or was my mind playing tricks on me?

I tried to remember details of the room.

A filthy mattress on the floor, cracked linoleum, stains on the walls. Cement or a stone cellar. Somewhere dirty. I was so desperate to make out every minute memory that they all washed together in my brain, tipping from reality to fiction until I wasn't sure I hadn't made it up at all.

I reached for the landline, ready to call Kel and tell him about the security screen, when I realized how silly it all sounded, because what was staring back at me now was exactly as it should be.

No room.

No bed.

No Tommy.

I wondered if whoever had taken Tommy would ask for a ransom next.

I backed out of the kitchen, fingers trembling as I tried not to imagine what kind of horror Tommy might be suffering right now. I backed into the master, the walls closing in as I sat at the edge of our bed, yanking the nightstand open only to find an empty space where my pistol should be.

It wasn't like Lenn to touch the sole weapon I kept in the house for protection, but what if it was *her* that needed protection from *me*?

CHAPTER FIFTEEN

Lennox
Two summers ago — early June

My fingers trembled as I gripped the steering wheel. The drive across town from Morrissey's to the trailer park was only five miles at most, but the shadows loomed heavy along the winding, tree-lined roads. I slowed multiple times when at the last minute a deer jumped out on a blind curve or lingered at the edges of my headlights.

I slowed down again when I turned onto Spruce Court, wondering what exactly I could say to my dad about creeping into the trailer in the middle of the night with the memory of a man's hands lingering on my skin. I'd waited so long, dreamed of the moment my husband's hands would bring me pleasure for the first time. And now this. Home didn't feel like a refuge, not with all the crazy chaos and vicious bickering between Mom and Dad. They'd be on me in a minute, my status as a latchkey kid long forgotten when they were sick of arguing with each other and turned their sights on me. As much as Dad gushed when my mom came to town, my heart usually sank. But as much as I hated to admit it, they knew me better than myself sometimes and going home would risk everything.

My car eased by Joe's Bar then, a local watering hole that only the darkest of drunks liked to visit. Joe's was a perfect fit for my dad, and apparently me tonight. I pulled into the parking lot and shifted into park. I opened the car door, my muscles as battered and weak as if I'd been hit by a bus. In the important ways, I guessed I had. Less than a week since the night in the pool house and I still couldn't shake the shame that coursed through me.

I pushed my hair behind my ears, hoping I looked halfway decent before sliding out. An ache throbbed behind my eyes as I crossed the dirt parking lot. I pushed the doors of Joe's open and a cloud of weed smoke greeted me.

I held my head high, eyes on the top-shelf whiskey, when a familiar voice called from the bar.

"Lenn!" Carl tipped a shot glass my way and waved me over.

I smiled, thankful for some semblance of normal as I crossed the dark barroom.

"Lenn? What happened?" Carl's genuine concern was cringeworthy.

I controlled my tears, strengthening my spine. "I was staying in the pool house when . . . when . . ." My mind searched for the words.

I had none.

If I told anyone about what really happened, far too many lives would change forever in this town. Our ambitions and goals were snaked together. The idea of starting an investigation into something that could unravel the very fabric of our small community was almost unbearable to me.

"Lenn — what pool house? Tell me, what did he do to you?"

"No, it's not that . . . It's just, I'm not sure what happened. Maybe it was all a dream."

He scoffed. "Looks like a nightmare."

I sank onto the bar stool at his side, gesturing to the bartender and asking for a double shot of rye whiskey. The bartender slid it across the bar a moment later, the aroma hot on my nostrils as I inhaled the smokey scent.

I slugged the shot back, the tingle erupting in my veins so welcome.

Carl was murmuring about a news story he was researching, and I was ordering another drink from across the bar.

My second arrived and Carl laughed, ordering himself another and doing a shot with me.

Within minutes of walking in, I felt like me again, the me before the night's horror.

"Remember the nights when our dads went out drinking together?" he said. "When they came home so drunk and happy they could hardly walk and sang and danced around the living room?"

Carl's eyes crinkled, his laughter flooring my senses. It felt good to forget. "Those are some of my favorite moments."

"They were crazy together."

"And apart."

Carl sipped his next tumbler of whiskey. "Reminds me of us."

"We're not half as crazy as they are," I said.

"Aren't we, Lenn? Don't we all just become our parents anyway?"

"I hope not." I giggled, sipping the amber liquid of my third double in as many minutes.

Carl's hand slipped to my knee and squeezed, his warm, comforting eyes shining across the dim light of the bar. "All of my moments with you are my favorites, you know?"

"Even back then?" I scoffed, visions of dirty pigtails and sandy toes came to mind.

"And even more now." His hand crawled up my thigh another inch before he smiled back at me softly. "It's been so long since we've just talked, you and I. It's good, Lenn, I've missed it. Truth be told, I miss everything about those days, especially when I had you."

I frowned, sensing the regret washing over him. We'd kissed once, the summer before Morrissey and I started dating, on the boardwalk after the fair with sticky cotton-candy lips. The sweet innocence of it felt like a million years away now.

"You look so sad, Lenn," Carl husked. "Let me kiss it better."

His words made me want to crumble into his arms. The pain of the last week was real, and the return to innocence Carl offered now was powerful.

My childhood best friend leaned in then, his lips dusting the corner of mine. My breathing hitched, hot tears clinging at my eyelids as the chug of the whiskey in my veins dulled my senses.

Both of Carl's hands crawled up my thighs then, dancing over my arms until he cradled my cheeks, pressing his lips to mine more firmly this time.

And I lost myself there.

I had to, I knew no other way.

I only wanted the pain to slip away, I wanted to be that girl in Carl's mind. The one with sandy feet and summer freckles without a care in the world.

The truth was, I'd never been that girl, but I liked that Carl thought of me that way.

And so I let his hands take away the pain, his lips kiss it better.

He dropped a fifty-dollar bill on the bar to cover our tab, locking his fingers in mine possessively and pulling me off my stool and against him. "I never stopped loving you, Lenn."

He swallowed my words with another soft kiss before leading me out of the empty bar and into the darkness. I left my car in the parking lot, sliding along the shadows of the streetlights alongside him as we walked the two blocks back to his trailer.

He slipped his palm between my thighs as I climbed the front steps, then his hands crawled under my shirt as he shouldered in the creaking metal door. He did like he'd promised, covering my skin in kisses before slipping his head under my sweatshirt and sucking the skin under my breasts.

I shuddered, the slow pulse of anxiety turning to arousal as the last few memories of my nightmare faded to black.

I knew all of Carl's secrets, and now he knew all of mine, or at least, what I'd allowed him to believe.

He guided me down the darkened hallway of his trailer, lips attached to mine as a familiar loneliness overcame me.

I slammed my eyes shut, fighting the memories of the roughening bites that had tracked across my mouth just days ago as *he'd* whispered about doing bad things, needing to tell someone, feeling trapped.

As *he'd* trapped me.

"I wish you would have given me another chance to prove that I can take care of you." Carl's words pulled me from my nightmares.

"It's not about that." I hated that he always went down this path with us.

"It is. It is for me. Give me another chance, Lenn. I still love you."

"Carl, we were so young."

Carl drew in a breath, fists clenching at his slides. "So I'm supposed to sit by and let you ruin your life with this asshole?"

"Morrissey's not an asshole," I muttered, too tired to fight.

"Prove it," he seethed. "Why does he make you so sad, Lenn?"

The pain faded to a dull ache as I began to dissociate the events of the night in my mind. They floated away, feeling more and more like a dream. Maybe I'd been foolish to trust anyone outside of this tiny trailer park bubble I'd grown up in.

"For you, I would do anything." He caught my chin with his fingers. "Just say the words."

His words cut me deeper than a serrated blade.

I pushed my hands over my head, wanting to drown myself in my hoodie and not exist anywhere, with anyone at that moment.

He'd known me long enough to know I'd always planned on saving myself for marriage. He'd told me he was doing the same. I hadn't thought he'd said it because of *me* then, but after his declaration of love . . .

It seemed funny now, the modesty he afforded me when another man's hands had crawled across my skin without my permission. I wouldn't — couldn't — say any more though, for fear of what Carl might be compelled to do.

I yearned for the moments of sweetness that had existed between us once upon a time, his lips tentatively pressed against mine when we were fourteen after a late-night game of spin the bottle.

So many of my firsts were with Carl, but not this.

"Take the sadness away, Carl . . ." I said, just above a whisper.

Carl's eyes bored into mine as we hovered at the doorway of his bedroom. "What?"

He wavered.

"Please." I hid the wince as I slipped a hand under my waistband and down between my thighs, testing the swollen flesh.

"What are you asking here, Lenn?" He shifted, Adam's apple bobbing at his throat. His eyes skipped down my body.

"Please."

"Lenn . . ." he croaked, eyes hooded as they skimmed the contours of my body. "I'll do whatever you ask. Always."

I swallowed the rock that had lodged in my throat as I felt some familiar pull between us. He searched my face. I draped my arms around his neck and pressed against him. His hands, slow and tentative, crawled under my tank top and up my bare back, his breaths ragged and quick at my ear.

My fingers trembled as I shuttered my eyes, imagining this was my first time, imagining the pain throbbing between my thighs wasn't from someone stealing the most precious part of me.

The whiskey still pumped through my veins as I breathed in the forgetting.

"Lennox . . ." Carl purred, a new fervor taking over his fingers as he grasped at my skin, pulling me to him and ushering us across the small thread-worn carpet, laying me back on his twin bed and holding himself above me. "Say it again."

I let his words hang in the air.

Do I want this?

No.

But I didn't want what had happened to me to happen either. But this, this would forever be my choice. The time I gave my everything to a boy I'd loved and trusted since childhood.

From that moment forward, Carl Meyer took my virginity and neither of us would ever tell a soul.

CHAPTER SIXTEEN

Morrissey
Fourth day: 6.07 a.m.

I let the mist wash over my face as I pushed harder on my morning run, appreciating the grinding crunch of the stone under my feet, anything better than the incessant peace that shrouded the Point. I reached the top of the knoll, seagrass whipping my knees before I slowed on the downslide; the dew-damp rocks were slick almost every morning of the year out here.

One loud gull squawked above my head before flying to the top of the boathouse, landing at the peak and watching me intently. I met the water's edge, pausing a moment to take in the low clouds that hung on the bay. The lighthouse was invisible behind the sea smoke, but for the light at the top winding around its axis on a timer.

Another gull shrieked and dive-bombed something in the bay, just out of my line of sight, before coming to land at the top of the boathouse next to the first. I walked down the beach, coming closer, before hopping on the dock that stretched out over the water. I could hardly make out the end, only the small glowing blue light mounted there.

I walked slowly down the worn slats, thinking in another year or two I'd need to replace these — something else we couldn't afford, not now. Maybe not ever. I hadn't wanted to admit it to Lenn, but we were way in over our heads on this — we had been from day one.

I reached the end of the dock, breathing shallowly as my eyes scanned the dozen or so feet of dark water that lapped at the pylons. Both gulls squawked and tussled over my head before they dive-bombed something bobbing just out of reach of my vision.

I stretched up on my tiptoes, squinting and wishing the mist would clear just another few inches. My eyes scanned the boathouse walls, catching sight of the fishing net and hook. I took the pole in hand, stretching it out the maximum twelve feet and catching the edge of something heavy.

Anxiety roared in my ears as I realized it was a boat — *my boat*. The dinghy that was normally hooked under the boathouse was now freely floating just off the dock, loose and . . . and . . . had it been missing the entire time? I hadn't thought to look. I used the hook to loop it over the edge, gulls going wild above me before a flash of baby blue came into view.

I dragged the dinghy in quickly, shocked to find my son's blanket, damp and dirty, in the bottom of the boat. I bent, lifting it to my nose and inhaling the scent.

Sour milk singed my nostrils.

I walked quickly back down the dock, stumbling by the time I reached the beach, and breaking into a full run by the time I was up the path and cresting the knoll. I wondered if there was any forensic evidence left on the blanket after it had sat out in the elements.

I wasn't sure how long it had been there or where its owner was. Fear was the only thing left throttling me forward, one horror-filled step at a time, as I imagined describing to Kel how I'd come across this.

By the time I reached the house I was surprised to find my mom's car sitting in the driveway. I ran Tommy's blanket through my fingers, folding it finally and setting it on the side table before opening the front door to greet my mom and search for my phone to tell Kel about Tommy's blanket.

Instead of finding my mom, though, today's newspaper sat on the counter and the scent of freshly brewed coffee floated through the house.

A WATER BABY COPYCAT AMONG US?

I stumbled when I read the headline.

I read it again.

The words didn't change.

My eyes scanned to the byline, annoyed to find that none was listed; the article was signed by an anonymous Thieves Cove resident.

"What sort of drivel is Carl printing now?" I grit, laying the newspaper open on the kitchen island before heading for the coffee pot to pour my first cup of the morning.

Mom walked in then and I remembered it was probably time I changed the keys. I hated that she helped herself to my life so easily. She looked like she'd been crying, stress straining her usually calm and measured features. Tommy was everything to her; she was his only healthy grandparent, and there nearly every day from his birth on. And her and Lenn had grown closer over the pregnancy and premature birth of our son. I could see the toll this was taking on her too; the way her hands shook as she sipped her coffee was enough of an indication that she was feeling this as deeply as I was. "I'm going crazy worrying about them, how was your night, honey?"

"I did my best. If it's not real life haunting me, it's my own thoughts as soon as my head hits the pillow." I nodded to the island. "Apparently we're front-page news."

"We?" Gigi Monroe arched one perfectly sculpted eyebrow. "What's a water baby?"

"Oh, who even knows? I haven't read it yet, but apparently it has something to do with Lenn."

I poured Mom a cup of coffee and passed it to her. Her normally coiffed hair was pulled back in a ponytail, the lines around her eyes more pronounced. She looked like she'd gotten about as much sleep as I had. "Hm." She pursed her lips as she read. "Is this for real?"

I shrugged. "It sounds like it never went anywhere from the way Kel tells it."

"Well—" her eyes scanned the text again — "this is all hearsay and speculation."

"How could you say that about Thieves Cove's finest news source?"

Mom frowned as she scanned the paragraphs. "Do they think this will help bring Tommy and Lennox back? I should get my lawyers on this. I'm not sure when the *Gazette* started printing opinion pieces on the front page."

"Since Carl decided to have it out for me."

Tommy's sweet face, nestled in a picture frame on the wall in the entry, caught my gaze then, his eyes bright and shining just like Lenn's used to.

Used to — it felt foreign, using the past tense.

I hadn't told my mother, or anyone, about the security camera blip with the baby on the mattress — I was convinced it was a me problem and I hadn't seen it at all.

"You don't really think Carl thinks you're behind her disappearance, do you?"

I shrugged, swallowing back the rest of my coffee. "He's hated me since the day Lenn and I got married. We were cool for a minute in high school, but since then I don't know what his problem is."

"Hm, I wonder if he has a thing for Lennox," Mom mused.

I raised an eyebrow. "You think?"

"Well, has he dated anyone else all these years?"

"I dunno," I deadpanned. "I don't really think about him and Lenn's never mentioned it."

"They were close in high school, weren't they? I used to see them once in a while, walking downtown or at the skate park next to the marina."

"I can hardly remember those days."

The filthy mattress on the grainy screen flashed in my head again. I couldn't begin to imagine what kind of horror my family may have witnessed, and because of that, I began to almost hope they'd just fallen over the dock, no horrendous kidnapping or murder — just slipped peacefully into the murky water and ceased to exist.

But why would Lenn be out in the middle of the night with our son? Had he woken up teething and she'd tried a walk to settle him down? It didn't make sense, not if I trusted my wife anyway. And the alternative, if I didn't trust her . . . well, I just couldn't fathom what that meant.

"It says here they're hoping DNA evidence will turn up in your case that might unlock clues to the original Water Baby case two decades ago. Let's hope that's true, because the alternative he's presenting is an active sex trafficking ring, funneling our children over the border. His words, *not* mine." She cast apologetic eyes at me.

"I don't even know what to wish for anymore, Mom."

She came over, hand at my back. "You wish for the little guy and his mama to come home soon and safely." Tears welled in her eyes.

"I didn't get much sleep last night. I feel like I'm losing my grip." I let my head droop, unable to even muster my next worst-case scenario.

"Honey, take care of yourself. You've been through so much, those reporters had blood in their eyes at the press conference, trying to twist your words and well . . ." She trailed off in disgust. "You take a pill to sleep if you need it."

I pushed a hand over my face. "Maybe I wouldn't have lost them if I'd had you here camping out."

She smiled sadly, cupping my face as tears streaked her cheeks. "You didn't lose them, Morrissey, they were taken from you, don't forget that. Nothing that you did caused this. Someone just has a very sick mind."

"Yeah," I hummed. "Should I toss this in the recycling bin?"

She folded the paper and tucked it away. "No, I'm going to keep that and do some of my own research about this Water Baby — anything to get our family back." Mom's eyes hung heavy with conflicting emotions before she wiped at a tear and smiled. "Our family has been through so much already."

"Thanks, Mom, for everything. I couldn't do any of this without you." I turned, headed for the couch in Lenn's office. I was just pulling the blinds for blessed darkness when I saw Kel's cruiser crest the knoll and stop at the front gate. "What now?"

I was back out in the kitchen before Mom even realized Kel was waiting. I buzzed the gates open, then opened the front doors wide and charged out into the driveway. He eased up slowly, eyes trained on me.

He opened his door, walking to me quietly.

I held still, frozen to my spot. "Kel?"

"Where were you last night, Morrissey?"

"What do you mean, I was right here."

"I'm going to need you to prove that."

"What? Why?"

My childhood friend's face turned dark. "A body was found in the bay."

I took a few steps back. "It's — is it . . . her?"

He shook his head quickly, eagle eyes never leaving mine. "A teenager. It's too soon to tell if it's related to Lenn and Tommy, but Morrissey . . . he was found floating in the bay around two this morning."

CHAPTER SEVENTEEN

Morrissey
Fourth day: 7.07 a.m.

"See?" I thrust a finger at the computer screen in Lenn's office. "I took your advice and installed another camera inside the house. That's the main hallway, Tommy's bedroom door is there—" I pointed — "and I was in my room all night."

I fast-forwarded the tape to the timestamp that was around the time I'd gotten up this morning.

"You look like shit, Morrissey." His eyes zeroed in on my hands on the video. "I have to have my tech guy look at this. Surveillance videos can be edited now, but from the looks of this tape you were right here last night, not getting much sleep."

"All night," I confirmed. I couldn't really account for the half-awake, half-sleeping hours, that dreamless place right before dropping off, where I had lines from "The Joker" cruising through my skull on repeat. I'd begun to wonder if I was having a mental breakdown — maybe the damn song had never played at all and I'd been so delirious I'd imagined the entire event.

"Can you email me a copy of that?"

“Sure.” I sent it off to him as he stood over my shoulder. “Is it possible for someone to hack my security cameras and show . . . something else?”

Kel arched an eyebrow. “Like what something else?”

“Anything. Maybe a glitchy connection or crossed wires somewhere. I’m just wondering if it’s possible.”

Kel considered quietly, eyes never leaving mine. “If I’ve learned anything in my line of work, it’s that anything is possible. I appreciate that you took my advice about the camera.”

“It’s a few days too short. I keep wondering if that one detail could give me more answers about what happened to her.”

His eyes scanned the papers strewn across my wife’s desk for the first time. “So, you didn’t see anything fishy last night around here?”

“No. My sleeping schedule is so messed up I hardly know if I’m comin’ or goin’.”

Kel sucked in a lungful of air, eyes blinking cautiously before he swallowed once and turned, perching his uniform hat on his head. “Helda organized the Lakeshore PTA for a search party across the bay. That woman has called in half a dozen tips in half as many days about your wife and boy. I finally put her on search party patrol to keep her busy. If you’re feeling up to it, maybe join them.”

I shuddered. “I don’t think that’s a good idea after the press conference. Do you think whoever took Tommy and Lenn did something to them and then killed themselves at my boathouse to make it look worse than it is?”

“Worse than it is?” The usual friendly smile was absent from his now sternly etched face. “Whatever works for you, Morrissey.”

I flinched inwardly with his words. Did he think I should be more involved? That I wasn’t doing enough? “Maybe Helda saw something, did you follow up on all of her leads?”

“Leads is a strong word.” Kel grunted. “She told me to look closer to home, whatever that means. You know she fancies herself a part-time psychic or some nonsense.”

"Really? I didn't know that." I thought a visit to Helda might be in order. Hadn't Lenn said once that her mom and Helda had been friends? "I meant to ask you—" I caught up to Kel as he walked through my kitchen to the front door — "what did the goat farmer say when you questioned him about the night Lenn vanished?"

Kel paused, squaring his shoulders and tipping his head. "Your neighbor, *Hank Rockwell*, was the one that found the body this morning. We can only assume it's connected with the disappearance of your family because of the proximity to your property. I'm working on a list of anyone that Lenn could have come into contact with over the last few years that may have left a bad taste. We haven't tracked down her mom yet and I sent a list of a few students at Central that I'm having campus security question, but so far nothing promising has turned up. I can put out an all-points bulletin for a person of interest, but I need a person of interest here, Morrissey. Did she mention any issues with a professor or roommate or counselor at school over the years?"

I shook my head, at as much of a loss as him.

"Well, a lot of weird things are happening on the Point lately and there's only two of you living up here right now." His tone was measured. "Have you taken any medication that could cause a lapse in memory?"

I thought of the sleeping pills. The night Lenn had laughed and asked if I was sleepwalking when I thought I'd seen her swimming. The label clearly stated they could cause weird dreams and night awakenings, that's why I'd weaned myself off of them. And why I'd installed security cameras facing *in*, just in case *I* was the one to be worried about in this scenario.

"Morrissey, don't jerk me around on this—"

"No. Nothing."

I couldn't have Kel barking up the wrong tree.

"Nothing to drink?"

"Only a few glasses of wine."

"The Hollows?"

"That's all we've been drinking since we moved in."

"Interesting." He made a few more notes on his pad. "Where do you keep the bottles stored?"

"We have a wine barn in back, your guys already searched it."

"You mind if I take a look?" Kel was already walking around the house.

I caught up, mentally scanning the space and hoping nothing was out of order.

"Have you ever had reactions to alcohol before? That pinot you gave me for Christmas was good but strong. Have you done the chemical analysis? Are you using oak or steel casks for your aging process?"

"I don't know." I flung the barn door wide and flicked on the light above the round table in the center of the room. "This is all Lenn's doing, she's had her head in books most nights learning the process. I don't know a thing about any of it, I just drink it."

"Nice." Kel circled a word on his pad and then closed and tucked it away in his breast pocket. *Sheriff Kendry* was stitched on top in gold thread.

It made me smile, thinking how we'd pitched high school baseball together, and now he was all but in charge of my fate. "You know anything about these tools?"

He pointed at more than a dozen winemaking tools in various stages of age and rust.

"Nope."

"Does it look like they're all there? Nothing missing?"

I shrugged, seeing each hung on a tiny rusted nail along the top third of the wall. "Looks fine to me."

"Did anyone else walk through here with you?"

"Nope."

Kel frowned again. "Does anything in here look off to you?"

I walked further into the room, eyes scanning the wooden barrels that lined one dark corner. Steel tabletop crushers and bottling equipment lined another wall, all untouched.

I turned, focusing my eyes on the smaller room we'd entered where Lenn did most of her daily work at the vintners table. Antique six-paned windows lined the opposite wall, and one very modern wine cooler with clear glass highlighted the last dozen remaining bottles of the Hollows wine.

"Everything looks normal."

"You think a tool belongs on that rusted tack?"

My gaze swung to where he pointed. A naked nail hung behind the door. "Maybe."

"Hm." Kel fished his phone out of his pocket and snapped a photo. "Keep your eye out for something that might hang there."

"Sure. Actually, I went for a run this morning and did find something. Maybe it's related to your body."

He paused, arching an eyebrow.

"Tommy's blanket, the one I put him to bed with that night, turned up off the boathouse. It's dirty, maybe it's been there since he went missing, maybe the forensics team can find something on it though."

"You found his blanket? Where is it now?"

"Up at the house, I'll take you." I waited for Kel, holding the barn door for him.

The stiff way he shuffled over the threshold was a reminder of the night on the bluff when we'd all walked away with our lives, Kel with a lasting memory every day.

Lenn and I never talked about that night again.

Compassion kills and lies connect us more than loyalty. The secrets we keep for each other hold the tightest bond. Only this time, our lies held stakes far steeper than they once did. This time, Kel was investigating my missing family, and I was walking on eggshells, wondering if I was next.

CHAPTER EIGHTEEN

Lennox
Two summers ago — late June

"I love you." His round eyes flicked to mine and I had to resist throwing up.

In a blink, the boy I hopelessly loved had turned into the man I could hardly stomach.

"I love you too." The words burned my lips. I hated myself for not believing them.

The lighthouse beam rotated in the distance as we sat on top of the Charger hood, shared double malt between us and stars burning up the sky above.

"Thank you for going with me to the funeral. This has been the hardest week of my life. I don't know what I would have done without you."

"There's no place I'd rather be."

I was saying the right things, but why didn't they feel right?

"You held my hand while I cried like a baby. I still can't believe he hung himself, it just doesn't make sense. My dad went from being this happy guy, singing in the car, to desperate and depressed? I don't believe it. I found some private investigators in Detroit that can look into it — maybe he was being blackmailed or something."

"Maybe."

"I went to the bank this morning. I inherited my trust this summer and I want to invest in you and me. In our future. Together. I know this seems rushed, but I've been thinking about it for a while. Marry me, Lenn. Please make me the happiest man alive."

With trembling hands, he slipped an oval diamond on my finger. Rows of cut stones framed the bigger center gem.

"Say yes, Lenn, and this is all yours."

He swept his hand behind us, the rolling hills of the Hollows and vineyard stretched in the distance.

"What?"

"This week has made me realize that we can't predict anything. All we can do is lean into the storms when they come and love what we have, because nothing is promised. *You* are all that I have, *you* are all that matters. Please, marry me?"

I gulped, my dreams so close, hovering at the edges of my eyelids like phantom tears.

"Yes."

CHAPTER NINETEEN

Morrissey
Fourth night: 11.05 p.m.

Kel's words about the goat farmer echoed on repeat for the next six hours.

And then another six after that.

I slept through the PTA search across the bay, I knew they wouldn't find her there. Instead, I woke up late to adrenaline pounding through my head. What the goat farmer had and hadn't seen consumed every pathway of my brain.

Before I knew what I was doing, and with enough energy coursing through my muscles to run a marathon, I stomped under the grape vines, crossing the width of the vineyard in a few short minutes before cresting the knoll, the farm and goat shed coming into view.

I reached the bottom of the hill and crossed the muddy puddles of his two-track driveway. The faint scent of wheat and oats and homemade bread floated from one of the open windows of the old farmhouse as I ducked beneath the ledge and allowed myself to be swallowed by the shadows. The goats bleated into the night, vibration echoing off the worn wooden timbers of the shed when a tall figure limped out of the front door of the house. I jumped, startling both of us and forcing a shout out of his mouth. He was on me in a moment, hand clutching the collar of my long-sleeve shirt, the stench of tobacco on his breath as he seethed, "What do you want?"

"I'm your neighbor, up over the hill. My wife and son went missing late last week and—"

"I know who you are." He didn't loosen his hold.

I grasped his hand and tore it off of me. "I came by to ask a few questions."

"You always wander around people's yards in the middle of the night?"

"Do you?" I blurted. "I mean, was that you I saw the other night down by my boat dock?"

He cleared his throat, turned away from me and walked the path to the shed. He swung the barn door wide when he reached it and dumped in a bucket of grain. A dozen or more goats clattered to the gate in a chorus of *baas*.

The way our house sat at the top of the knoll shielded us from a lot of this blatting noise, but what if it hid secrets too?

"I wasn't anywhere near your boat dock the night your wife went missin' if that's what you're asking. Same thing I told the sheriff."

I fell into step beside him. "Do you always do your chores at night?"

He paused near the corner of his house, a dim spotlight angled haphazardly illuminating one side of his face. I wasn't prepared for what came next when he turned fully to me.

Scars, violent gashes and marled skin stretched from the corner of his lip to beyond his sharply angled cheekbones. "So what if I do?"

I averted my eyes. "Have you ever seen anything suspicious up at my place, around my vines or the dock?"

"Only you and your wife."

I took in his words, trying to structure my next ones carefully. "When's the last time you saw my wife out after dark?"

He turned away, scooping another bucketful of grain and then returning to the now quieter goats. "Most every night until she disappeared."

"Every night?" My blood ran cold. "Did you tell Kel that?"

"Should I?" His good eye angled to mine, suspicious in the silver moonlight.

"Maybe. Did anything about what she was doing seem suspicious?"

"Is anything about what you're doing in the middle of the night at my place suspicious?"

Irritation pricked at my insides. "It's my boat dock." He only grunted. "Maybe I should ask what you were doing this morning to find a body floating just off my waterline?"

Silence breathed heavily between us, the incessant ring of the crickets and tree frogs suddenly deafening in the air.

"I collect fresh water for my goats every night down at the shore, been doin' it for years, only way I can survive on this property without a well to pump from."

"You don't have running water?" I thought of the irony, us surrounded by so much, and him still forced to live like he was in the great depression.

"Never have. Well-driller sunk his pipe, but the money ran out before we struck gold."

The bitterness lacing his words struck a chord. I hated to admit that I didn't know much about this man that we'd set up our dream right beside — hadn't paid him a thought beyond the eyesore that was his rambling shed and even more derelict farmhouse.

"I own the thirty-foot easement down to the shore, it's written into the title of this place. I know your fancy realtor came over tryin' to strong-arm me about my path to the water bein' on your property, but like I told her — if she steps foot on my property again without checking first at the courthouse, I can't be held responsible for what's required to protect my property."

"Protect your property?" I gulped, thinking I was more out of my league with this guy than I'd thought. "Are you threatening me?"

"Do I need to be more clear?"

I was fuming now. "I don't care about your goats or your damn water, I care about my wife and my son and—"

"Well, may do you good to know I saw someone buryin' somethin' up the likes of your hill the night she went missin'."

"What?" His words acted like cold ice on my system. "Can you take me there?"

He grunted, pouring a bucket of fresh water into the goat trough before setting it on the ground. "I'll show you, alright, and then I don't want to see your face again."

I followed quickly along as he climbed the hill.

He may have had a slow ambling gait when he walked around the farmyard, but hiking uphill now, he moved with agile speed and strength. My eyes stretched the breadth of his shoulders and I found myself wondering if Lenn could take a guy like this in hand-to-hand combat if she had to.

He stopped abruptly at the top of the hill, eyes scanning the vineyard quickly before he walked the crest and seemed to almost count off his steps. He stopped at the industrial grape crusher, before slanting his chin to the left and counting off five more strides. "You got a shovel?"

My eyes scanned the ground, noticing for the first time it was freshly tilled right around where his dirty old boots stood, and only a few yards from the mouth of the hopper that fed the crusher. My stomach swam, my head spinning as I tried not to think about all the things I might find if I started digging.

Was I ready?

"Well?" he barked, making me jump.

"You saw someone burying something here the night Lenn went missing?"

"Sure did."

"W-why didn't you dig then? Or tell Kel to dig? Or . . . or why would I even believe you now? Maybe this is a trick to throw me off the scent, and really you know more than you're letting on." My hands were shaking now, fight or flight solidifying in my veins like hot lava. "I . . . I think if you didn't tell Kel this, then there's more you're not saying." I knocked him into the crusher, holding my hand at his papery throat. I sank the pad of my thumb into the hollow of this neck and seethed, "I think you need to tell me everything you think you saw right now or I'll mangle another part of you in this crusher."

I locked my grip at his wrist and forced it down the chute. His muscles trembled, and I couldn't see his eyes, but I imagined they were laced with fear.

"Tell me!" I screamed, forcing his fist closer to the blades. They weren't turning, but it would only take me a moment to reach around the protective shield and hit the big red *go* button. Something desperate inside of me, something that had been caged, threatened to burst free and I thought about hitting the button just to scare him into confessing everything to me.

"Why don't *you* tell *me*? You've been harassing me since you moved up to the Point, why don't you tell me where she is? I told the police where to look — told them to check the boathouse and the bay. I knew something was wrong when I saw the two of them down there that night."

"Who? You saw who?"

"How much do you know about your wife? What would send her out into the bay, swimming laps like a pro under the cover of darkness?"

My head throbbed.

"Where is she?" I grit at his ear.

He didn't speak, and it pissed me off, but then the strong odor of urine filled the night air a moment later.

I sucked in sick breaths and closed my eyes as I wondered what I was doing. Maybe this was all a bad dream, maybe I was sleepwalking or, or . . .

"I told you all you need to know."

Fear flooded my synapses before I let go of the old man, pushing myself away from him and falling back onto the ground he'd just told me might contain the remains of my dead wife or son.

The old goat farmer stumbled away from the grape crusher, the limp of his leg worse than when we'd climbed the ridge.

He disappeared seconds later.

I was left on my knees, alone under my grape vines, wondering if any of the last few moments had even happened.

CHAPTER TWENTY

Lennox
Two summers ago — early July

"You know I hate this." Carl's arms came around my waist.

The night before my wedding to Morrissey, I was in another man's arms.

All of us had been through so much in the few short weeks since all of our lives had fallen apart together.

"I know . . ." I offered a small smile and let him place a tender kiss on my forehead. "Thank you for . . . everything."

Silent beats passed between us as I thought back to the night that had forged our now unshakable bond. We were family, he and I, born of blood and bone. I couldn't explain it, those worst moments of my summer were a blur, and forgetting them was all I'd ever wanted to do in the first place.

Was bringing Carl into it my very best decision? Of course not, but I had nowhere else to turn.

The relationship Morrissey and I had had evaporated when he woke up the same morning of my rape to find his dad hanging from a beam in the pool house. He'd come to find me, assuming I was already up because "The Joker" by Steve Miller was echoing through the speakers on repeat.

Instead he'd found his own brand of horror.

I hadn't answered his calls that day. I was dealing with my own nightmare, totally unaware of his until the headline in the paper the next morning reported Frank Monroe's suicide. I'd gulped back tears for the man I'd known, the man Morrissey would now be forced to become, our shared innocence bitch-slapped by shared circumstance.

He hated that song now and I hated this town, its quiet beauty and wild nature more oppressive than it had ever been. The constant drizzle and mist hovering on the water kept a cold death grip on the people around it.

"You remember that pact we made when we were twelve behind the baseball diamonds?"

A sad smile turned my lips. "How could I forget? In the unlikely event we're not married by twenty, we'll marry each other. Twenty — what a lot of time we gave ourselves to find *the one*."

"I never needed more time." His tone was soft. "I still stand by my word, Lenn."

His words cracked me wide open.

He'd given and I'd taken so much.

"We were kids, Carl." I wiped my eyes. "We were all just kids."

"And we're not anymore." His eyes dashed to the ceiling. "It's going to be hell walking you down the aisle tomorrow. I'm kicking myself for saying yes when you asked."

"Thank you for saying yes, Dad wouldn't have it any other way. He trusts you more than anyone when it comes to me." I thought of my father, now mostly bound to his wheel-chair after his kidneys had taken another dive.

"You know . . . I still wonder what would have happened if I'd hauled you away that night you came back to my house. I would have loved the hell out of you, Lenn." I could hear the emotion throbbing in his words.

I still pained him, the flame he held for me as bright as ever.

"Carl," I whispered, "please don't do this."

"All I've ever wanted was to love you for who you are, not for who you want to be someday."

"Carl." Regret strained my vocal cords. We hadn't spoken of that night since. It had been festering, and as much as I'd wanted to avoid it, he'd been anxious to talk about it. I could see it in the way he tensed his muscles and his eyes tracked me across a room, but before he could make his move, I'd said *yes* to Morrissey.

"I've lived with regret since that day. It wouldn't be right of me if I didn't say it out loud. I've never judged you, Lenn — have you thought maybe that's why you haven't told him, because he might leave if he knew what we did?"

"No, no!" Rage balled my fists. "That's not true. He loves me. You don't know it, he shows it differently than you do."

"By sending you broken and sad into my arms in the middle of the night?" Tears swam with his words as a headache pounded at my frontal lobe. So many little white lies. "Gold digger doesn't look good on you."

What had I created? The boy that had helped me clean my scrapes and taught me to ride a bike without hands now uttered vile words that settled in my core like a thousand bee stings. "Please, that's not what this is . . . I love him."

He shook his head in disgust. "I close my eyes at night and all I see is you. I just want you back."

"You never had me, Carl . . ." I couldn't take it anymore, the fear that the bubble I'd built the last few months of my life on was now threatening to pop with every one of his well-aimed arrows. "You promised you would never tell, you promised you would do anything for me. *Anything*."

"And I did, didn't I?" His rage was at a tipping point, rage born of the pain I'd caused. "I've kept your dirty little secret so well that Morrissey *fucking* Monroe still believes you're the innocent little wife he's been waiting for, but the virgin white dress doesn't match the girl wearing it, does it?"

"Carl—"

"What next, Lenn?" he rumbled. "What will you ask of me next?"

CHAPTER TWENTY-ONE

Morrissey
Fourth night: 12.42 a.m.

Dirt caked under my fingernails as I dragged my palms through the wet earth, desperate pants racking my frame as I dug. Salty tears mingled on my cheeks as the heavy fog that often blanketed the bay mixed with the thick air that clung to the cove.

My arms grew weaker and heavier as I continued to dig. Faint wisps of silver and the regular rotation of the automatic lighthouse beam lit the darkness beyond the roofline of our house.

Our house.

My house.

Tommy's childhood home.

If I found anything in this hole that pointed me to my wife, I vowed right there I would sell this property and move. I would probably have to anyway — I couldn't afford the place more than a few months unless I managed a miracle.

Drops of rain weighted my hair before my fingers hit a scrap of white cloth. I froze, heart lodged in my throat as my fingers felt around the familiar white linen. I dug quicker then, praying I wasn't about to find what I thought I might find.

The remains of my wife.

"Lenn . . ." I dug fast, working around the edge of the pile, relieved to discover it wasn't much bigger than the size of a few footballs wrapped in what looked like one of the top sheets to our bed. Lenn had spent a fortune on sheets after we'd bought the new California king-sized mattress to fit the custom built-in headboard and cherry wood frame. She would rather die than drag them through the dirt like this unless, unless . . .

I grunted when the dirt turned to clay as my twenty-inch-deep hole turned into a mudslide. I wedged the bundle free, falling back onto my backside and clutching the sheets to my chest. I could feel something inside, not heavy, but heavy enough that I needed to investigate as soon as I could.

I swallowed, thick clouds hanging overhead darkening the sky. I stumbled to my feet, walking quickly down the rows of vines until I reached the wine barn. I couldn't bring this into the house with the cameras everywhere when I didn't know what this contained.

It didn't even cross my mind to call Kel. It should have. It really should have. If I wasn't holding my own ugly truths close to my vest, maybe I would have, but I had to know what I was facing — I couldn't stand another surprise.

I pushed inside the wine barn, letting the door swing wide and flicking on the small bulb that hung over the old vintner's table that Lenn had scoured local flea markets to find. I could see her silhouetted here in the sunset, only a few nights before she vanished, while Tommy crawled in the clover at the doorway just beyond her feet. I winced at the memory as my hands unwrapped the organic California king sheets, fingertips settling on the soft deckled edges of moleskin journals.

I gulped, letting them fall free on the bench and spreading dozens and dozens out with my hands, my eyes wild as I considered them all greedily.

The first was dated in the top corner just a few weeks ago.

I gulped, checked another. Still, a few weeks ago.

Another, a year ago.

Another, three months.

Another, two years.

The chicken scratch spun through my vision, my brain unable to process most of the words as I saw what looked like her almost-familiar handwriting, but with a fevered edge. Angles that were sharper than usual. Angrier, more frantic.

The handwriting of a mad woman.

CHAPTER TWENTY-TWO

Morrissey
Fifth day: 6.52 a.m.

Reading her journals felt like meeting a stranger for the first time.

The voice was familiar, but with a ravaged edge. I didn't know the tortured woman who'd written these pages, the self-annihilating scorn she bestowed on herself was the voice of a person in pain . . . or worse, a soul deranged.

I gulped, fingering the last few pages of the journal as my eyes swallowed stories about Carl pushing her about something, and the guilt she held for the secrets she kept from me.

I turned to the last page, surprised to find the writing flowing off the paper, and at least half a dozen pages missing from the back of the notebook. I could see where they'd been torn from the binding, the edges of ink from her sloppy writing still visible at one torn corner.

I slammed the journal closed, picking up another from the stack, one dated over a year ago, and rifling through it. I was looking for something closer to the date we'd gotten married — this seemed to be the time her writing took on a more frantic lilt. I picked up another journal, eyes scanning for the date I was interested in.

This one, dated only a week after our wedding, started with an argument between her and Carl and his refusal to accept the miscarriage.

The miscarriage.

When had Lenn ever had a miscarriage?

She'd surprised me with her pregnancy only two months into our marriage, and she'd claimed to be a virgin that afternoon we'd picnicked by the lighthouse . . . how was it possible that my wife had had a miscarriage and I didn't know about it? Our lives had always been intertwined in the years before now.

And why was it that Carl knew the most private thing about my wife, while I was kept in the dark?

Anger simmered to life inside of me.

What other secrets had Lennox been hiding?

I tossed the journal back on the pile, pushing away from the stool I'd been hunched on. My eyes fell to the sheet, a dark red stain now visible in the early morning light. "Lenn, what aren't you telling me?"

And then a horrible thought crossed my mind.

What if Lenn had done all of this — created this kidnapping — as a diversion for something else? Or worse, what if she and Carl had orchestrated something far more sinister, starting way back from before our wedding? Maybe she'd been cheating on me the entire time, my dumb ass none the wiser as she told me I would be her first and her last.

She'd mentioned moments of feeling oppressed and suffocated out here on the Point alone with me. I thought I'd given her the best wedding gift when I'd purchased the Hollows for her, when really, had it led to our destruction?

Too much isolation can go to a woman's head, I remembered Fawn saying.

Was she right? And Mom too, when she'd begged me not to buy this big rambling house? I'd been so driven by my love for Lenn and her happiness, I hadn't much considered the other alternatives. Like that Lennox had been lying to me all along to get into my family's bank account, and now this, her ploy to take what was left, and my sanity along with it.

Was my wife having an affair from day one?

I stumbled out of the wine barn, slamming the wooden door behind me with a thunk as my eyes blurred, Lenn's haunted scrawl tattooed behind my eyelids. The moonlight played shadows with the grape trellises, clouds hanging low and casting empty black holes along the rows.

"What the hell . . ." I squinted, eyes playing tricks as a hooded figure dashed across the knoll. I took a few cautious steps down the first row of grapes, unwilling to run down the row to discover if my eyes were playing tricks, knowing that by the time I reached the end it could be a trap. I came around the edge, wishing I'd hung a few solar lights out here for security, approaching the grape crusher from the back angle.

I was probably seeing things — most definitely probably — but it was hard to say with the way my vision was running together after reading Lenn's frantic handwriting for the last few hours. I cursed myself for not bringing the journals into the house to read, but I hadn't wanted to . . . what? Know the truth?

Maybe I'd been fearing what they might contain all along. Or, more likely, that security camera turned indoors was giving me pause.

CHAPTER TWENTY-THREE

Lennox
Two summers ago — late July

"Carl, hi."

My former best friend's smile was dark. He arched an eyebrow, eyes crawling up and down my body, as if every time he saw me, he needed the visual reminder of what we'd done that one night I refused to speak of again.

Until now.

"Mrs. Monroe," Carl cooed. "Long time, no see."

I gulped, scanning his cart full with bags of chips and stacks of frozen food. I imagined him all alone in that trailer, playing video games and pickling his liver with alcohol and preservatives.

"Oh, what's this?" He narrowed his eyes on the boxes in my basket. One box of each of the three brands the grocery store offered. "A pregnancy test?"

I clamped my mouth shut. The truth was, I didn't need the tests, I'd stopped in here to confirm the other two at home.

I was pregnant, and now I didn't know what to do.

"Is it mine?" His tone rang with disdain. "Or is it Mr. Monroe's? I keep forgetting, you *are* a married woman now."

My heart sank at his choice of words. Bile rose in my throat as I thought the unimaginable.

"I don't know what you expected after that night, but I know I did not expect this," he sneered. "The Monroe family has you lookin' tired already, Lenn. Too bad."

I winced, his vicious side surfacing more and more these days. It was then I realized he'd imagined that we would really be together after the night I pretended to give him my virginity. Maybe it had been my most selfish move, but the alternative felt far worse.

I'd seen him only a few times in passing around town since the wedding, and now here we were, face to face under the worst of circumstances.

Me, caught red-handed with a basket of pregnancy tests and another nightmare on my hands.

The worst part, I'd done the math six ways from Sunday. There was no chance this baby was Morrissey's, which meant that on our wedding night, I'd already been pregnant.

"Carl." I pulled him down a narrow aisle.

His lips twitched at my touch. "We could be together. I would raise this baby with you."

His words cut like a knife. "No . . . I'm a Monroe now . . ."

He laughed loudly, drawing attention to us. "Got your dream then, huh? Big fat bank account in a big fat house up on the Point. Didn't take you long to insert yourself into that family, did it? Don't ever speak that name in my presence. I hate him, Lenn, I hate all of them, because it would kill me to hate you."

His words crushed me because I'd crushed him. The boy who thought he really, truly loved me, and I'd trampled all over those feelings just to forget one awful night. I was the monster here, no one else.

"Can't you cut them some slack? You heard what happened—"

"I don't give a fuck if his dad shot up half the town, that family is toxic. He runs off with the three hundred pensions and hangs himself in his cushy pool house while half of his former employees are trying to avoid living on the street."

I winced, the truth of his words hitting home. "I know . . . Dad didn't even go to the funeral."

"Why would he? Frank Monroe stole everything your dad earned. I don't know how you break bread with those criminals. Did you see the obituary in the paper? It took up half the front page. If I'd have been in charge of what went to print that day, it would have been a different story altogether."

"Carl, he employed half the town for the last two decades. Sometimes businesses go under, it happens."

"And then he stole every last dime he promised them."

I swallowed. "I won't listen to you hate on the Monroes."

"Well, what did you come here for then? To flaunt your little bastard child in my face?"

"Carl, please."

"What, you want my help? You need a ride to the abortion clinic, Lenn?" he sneered. "Maybe ask your Richy Rich husband."

"Carl, stop." I wrung my hands, hating myself for the thoughts that had been circling my brain. "I just . . . don't know what else to do."

Carl's body went rigid. "So you hardly talk to me for a month, and the next time I see you, you ask for my help?"

"No, no, I guess, I just . . ." I shoved my fingers into my hair. "I can't handle this. I really can't."

Carl's eyes hardened. "So what? Do you want me to beat you up? Throw you down my trailer steps until you're bleeding? What are we doing here, Lenn?"

Hysteria was shaking me now. I hadn't told a single person. "I'm fucking losing it at the Point. I'm not asking for help, okay? I guess I just thought . . ."

He shook his head. "Isn't there some morning-after pill you can take now?"

"And buy it where? From Sherry that works at the pharmacy and went to high school with Morrissey's mom? It's fine, I'll figure it out."

I pressed a hand to my eyes, mind whirling. Had I really asked what he was suggesting? It didn't feel like that to me, it only felt like I wanted my life back from the moment before my choice was taken from me.

Did that make me a bad person?

I was already exiting the aisle, Carl following me as he uttered, "I told you once I would do anything for you, Lenn. I still mean that today, even if I am mad at you."

I stopped to look into his hollow eyes, normally so vibrant, now dark and angry. Had I brought that storm cloud to his life? Without a doubt.

Thieves Cove suddenly didn't feel like home anymore.

"Whatever you need me to do, I will, Lenn."

CHAPTER TWENTY-FOUR

Morrissey
Fifth day: 10.24 a.m.

I'd come to fully believe that Carl was the father of the baby that Lenn had miscarried — when it had happened, I had no idea, and didn't really want to know. The more I thought about the things Lenn didn't tell me, the more I drove myself insane about the things I still didn't know.

I shuffled in the weathered Adirondack chair, my eyes scanning the gray mist that hovered over the dark waves. Lenn talked of feeling suffocated by the constant cloud cover that hung over the Point. I thought she'd loved that about it.

Had it driven her to madness, forced her to disassociate with the memories we were making here? This was the very bay where she'd been found as a baby, according to Kel — had trauma from that time forced her into the lake now, purposefully ending her life? I'd never expected my father's suicide, had Lenn suffered the same fate?

I didn't think so, I was almost sure of it, but then I remembered the night she'd come in off the beach, hair soaked and the smell of sand on her skin. She said she hadn't been swimming, blamed it on my sleeping pills playing tricks on me, and I'd accepted her explanation happily, but now, I wasn't so sure.

Mom stepped out on the porch then, silently refilling my coffee mug and dropping the rolled newspaper in my lap. I was secretly grateful for her morning coffee deliveries. A touchstone with reality. I uttered a thank you, my mind already returning to Lenn and her mysterious journals.

How had the love of my life changed under my eyes and I hadn't realized it? Not even for a second? Had there been signs? Was my head too far up Titan Transport's messy financials that I'd neglected my family?

My gaze cut across the bay, crawling past the tiny fishermen's cabins that lined the opposite shoreline. I thought of the figure I'd seen hovering at the edge of our boathouse, how the stretch of the shoulders and the length in the legs were familiar.

I could no longer tell down from up, but a new wave of awareness settled over me. My wife had lied to me at least once.

Maybe the only people I could rely on were right here in this house, right now.

I took a sip of my hot coffee, setting the mug on the deck railing and unfolding the newspaper.

My mouth dropped when I read the front headline.

"Mom."

"Yeah, honey?" She sing-songed a moment later. Her eyes fell on the headline and she breathed, "Oh."

TORRID AFFAIR REVEALED IN WATER BABY 2.0 CASE

"Torrid affair? How could Carl let this go to print?"

"Carl just made himself an appointment with my fist."

"Oh, Morrissey, stop. Your dad and I didn't raise you that way."

"Mom!" I gripped the paper — a grainy photocopy of the torn pages of the journal I'd just spent last night reading were staring back at me. My wife's darkest secret, printed for all in Thieves Cove to see.

How had Carl gotten his hands on Lenn's journals? Had the goat farmer mentioned his suspicions to someone, and they'd found them before I had? Did Kel have some of these in his possession and someone at the department leaked them? But then why bury the rest of them? Unless . . . the journals were never real to begin with, just a plant to throw the investigation off. And how would it look to the police department now if I suddenly showed up with newly discovered evidence about Lenn's supposed affair — would Kel think I'd planted the journals with Carl to smear Lenn's reputation?

"Well, it's all lies anyway. They redacted the name of the other party. Doesn't that prove something?" Mom tore the paper from my hands but I caught her before it ripped.

"Mom—" I choked on the next part. "I think it's true."

"You don't think . . . ?"

I shook my head. "I wouldn't have yesterday morning, but after what I found . . ."

"What did you find, Morrissey?" Mom's voice was suddenly urgent, eyes pinned to mine.

"Journals, with pages missing that look just like that one."

"What do they say?"

"I'm too afraid to read," I replied as Mom snatched the paper from my hands, then walked across the deck to gain distance from me as her eyes scanned the paragraphs.

"Oh, for Heaven's sake." She scoffed, turning the page and continuing to read. She folded the paper neatly, then tossed it on the patio table. "Are you sure that's her handwriting?"

"I wish it wasn't."

She lingered at my side, eyes washing over the horizon before she finally *tsked* to herself and turned back to the house. She paused at the French doors. "That paper is salacious and biased. I'm ashamed to say your father and I donated to them numerous times over the years. I'm not sure what the world has come to when it becomes appropriate to run something like that — so, so distasteful about a missing—"

"Mom!" I cut her off, recognizing the shrill tone that meant Gigi Monroe was about to lose her cool. "Think about it — where did Carl get those pages?"

Silence opened up between us, only the cool September wind moving in the minutes that unfolded. Mom cast her gaze to her feet, wiping at a tear before shaking her head. "She's just not the woman I thought she was."

"You and me both."

"Honey, I'm so sorry, I've been so selfish just thinking about . . ." She sniffed, dropping to her knees and clutching at my hand. "I can't imagine what this must be like for you. If those journals are real, I . . . I just want you to know I'm here to help you, however I can. You're all I have left now that your dad is gone. Lennox may have made mistakes but we'll honor both her and your dad's memory by doing our best. I just pray we can find that little boy. Both of them."

I sighed, mind still firing off with all of the implications of Carl's latest stint in print. "You know what this means, Mom?"

"Hm?" She was busy wiping her tears and straightening her hair.

"It means everyone in this town is going to assume I found out about the affair that my wife was having, so I killed her."

"Morrissey, no, the people in this town know you, they'd never dream that—"

"They don't know me any more than I knew Lenn." I stood in front of the chair. "I pray Tommy doesn't find this someday."

"Oh God." Mom covered her mouth. "You're right, what if it says explicit things in there, things that were said after they . . . and a fight they must've had later . . . Morrissey, what can we do? I won't have your father work so hard to build the Monroe name only to tarnish his legacy after he's gone."

"Mom, I'll figure it out, please don't worry."

The alarm signaling someone at the gate buzzed through the house. I glanced at the CCTV and recognized Kel's cruiser and groaned.

"Kel. God knows what wonderful news he's bringin' with him today."

"Maybe it's good news," Mom offered brightly.

I surreptitiously rolled my eyes as I opened the door to find my childhood friend frowning back at me. "You've seen the paper?"

I left the door open and turned, angling for the coffee pot. "I'm sure I'm the last one. I just saw it for the first time a few minutes ago."

"Did you know?"

"What?" I barked. "About the affair?"

He waited, eyes unwavering.

"I found out recently," I grit.

"How recently?"

I didn't answer, wondering how much I should and shouldn't relay. "Let's just say, I had a heads-up before the news hit the headlines."

"Morrissey, that's not good." He stepped closer, removing his uniform hat and setting it on the table. "I did a little digging this morning after I saw the headline, thought it was suspicious already after that Water Baby article the other day, so I pulled the security footage from the camera mounted on the electrical pole outside the newspaper office the night Lenn went missing. I know you said she dropped something off for the charity event, but can you think of any reason why they might have argued that night?"

"This is the first time you've pulled the security footage from the newspaper? You didn't do it before now — like, when I told you where she'd been right before she went missing? Carl is the most suspicious sonuva—"

"Morrissey, of course I didn't — we're all friends here. Why would I have a reason to suspect anything? He said all was normal when she left, and I believed him, just like I believed you."

I gnashed my teeth together. "Argued?"

"Fighting like an old married couple — he grabbed her wrist at one point and she jerked away. You could tell she was crying. They were out in the parking lot for about twenty minutes before he tried to hug her and she pushed him off and walked to her car."

"And that's it?"

"She pulled out and came home. I checked the other known security footage between here and your house — her car was time-stamped on them like you'd expect — and then she arrived home, which is corroborated on your security system." He gestured to the grainy camera in the corner that showed a gridded screen with various angles around the property.

I thought of the grainy flash of a dirty mattress, a small baby sleeping soundly on top. My chest ached.

"I can't think of any reason her and Carl might argue." The lie burned on my lips, the evidence of their affair burning up the pages of the journals I'd just read. Torrid didn't begin to cover it. From the start, he seemed more into her than she him, her tone regretful while his hopeful, if not pushy. Maybe I should have turned over the journals to Kel, but he already had the evidence he needed to investigate Carl, why did he need mine?

Unfortunately, the pages printed in the newspaper were the more scandalous parts anyway, the ramblings of a woman I never knew.

"You want a cup of coffee?" I gestured. "It's the only thing keeping me alive these days." I gestured.

Kel shook his head, eyes crossing the room to the CCTV screen again. "You know my crew and I have been spending all hours on Lenn's case, and then this body was found in the bay."

"Have you confirmed it's murder?"

"Suspicious circumstances." Kel put his hat back on his head, backing away, before lowering his tone. "I have to ask you, Morrissey, did you kill your wife because you found out she loved another man?"

"She didn't love him, Kel."

His eyes shot up in surprise. "Sure about that?"

"She didn't. Whatever happened, it wasn't love. I know Lenn had secrets, but she couldn't fake what we had."

"Well, you say that, but I've got important people breathing down my neck about bringing you into the station for a proper interview."

"You mean on the record? Haven't we been from the start?"

"I haven't been recording anything. Technically, anything you say to me out here wouldn't hold up in court if, you know . . . well, it'd be your word against mine."

"I see."

"Some even think you may be connected to the body that floated ashore just off of your boathouse . . ."

"The same area my batshit crazy goat farmer of a neighbor lurks to 'collect water for his goats.'" I made air quotes around that last half. I was being dramatic, but I was feeling it. Feeling his scrutiny and distrust. "I know you're doing your job, but stop fishing, Kel, you know us."

"I do." Kel reached the doorway, shaking his head once. "I know all of you very well."

CHAPTER TWENTY-FIVE

Lennox
Two summers ago — early August

I tucked my new moleskin under the deckchair, folding it under the edge of the fuzzy blanket before descending the steps into the dark mist. The lighthouse shimmered across the bay, silver moonlight glinting off its windows and lending a smokey quality to the fog shrouding the water.

The Point was growing on me. I'd lost myself in the tragedy of our lives for a while, but writing my feelings down each day seemed to help.

When I reached the edge of the shoreline, I dipped my toes through the foaming bubbles, slipping my swim coverup over my shoulders and depositing it at my feet before stepping deeper into the surf. I hummed with pleasure as the water enveloped my skin, washing away my worries as my hands cupped my belly.

Confused tears spilled onto my cheeks before I lay back in the water, allowing myself to float with the current. We'd only been in this house a few weeks. The knowledge that I was newlywed and pregnant with a baby that wasn't my husband's was soul crushing, but the possibility of crushing his heart with the truth ruined me more.

I couldn't bear the thought of keeping this baby, or not keeping it. I didn't think I had the heart to confess the sins of the man that my husband loved so much and held so dear to his very legacy.

Legacy. So important to one family, so foreign to another.

And Carl. Somehow it felt like I'd devastated my childhood best friend, wrapped him in my toxicity and cast him aside in favor of my life with Morrissey. The only thing I'd been able to feel in those moments was pain; I only hoped one day he could forgive me for turning to him to ease it.

Our limited interactions had been so horrible since he'd walked me down the aisle and then practically verbally assaulted me beforehand, but I'd held it together because I'd seen the pain in his eyes. Recognized the horrible mistake I'd made. Every time he'd caught my gaze at the ceremony or the reception, I'd felt the pressure of his judgment, regret soaking my bones at the memory of our one fevered night shared in his bed. The pleading in his body language when he'd given me a hug, his dry kiss on my cheek before he turned and walked away. His previously well-aimed words had already left their mark. I'd been rattled by his silence and avoided him ever since.

I'd had no other direction then. And the fact that Carl knew too much sat uneasy with me now. What if he decided to confess my darkest sins to the only man I'd ever loved? What if Morrissey left me when he realized this baby wasn't his? And he would. My secrets wouldn't stay buried forever, no matter how much I wanted them to vanish.

Marrying Morrissey had felt like a fresh start. A rebirth. But the truth of it was, I'd never felt more trapped.

I turned in the water, using my new swim stroke to slice the gentle waves and swim a little deeper out. I knew there was a sandbar nearby, I had only to swim a dozen or so feet over my head before I could touch the bottom again. I gulped, fear gripping my limbs as I neared the drop-off underwater that would leave me out of touch and floating free.

The absolute fear of the depths of nothingness below sent terror spiking through my veins before I used my butterfly stroke to swim backward to shore, propelling myself away from the abyss again. My goal to cross the stretch of open water to the lighthouse wouldn't be accomplished tonight.

But at least I wouldn't die trying. Not tonight anyway.

I reached the shallow shore, toes digging into the fine grains of sand as I climbed out of the water, soaked and satisfied. I was just pulling my coverup over my shoulders and untucking my hair from the tightly wound bun, when Morrissey stepped out onto the deck.

I froze, uncomfortable with him seeing me like this, right now.

And then I realized how silly I was being, keeping this one small secret when I had such a large one looming.

I gulped, sick of overthinking my moves, then swept up the journal and blanket and wound my way up the sandy path that led to the back of the house. From this vantage point I could see his eyes searching the yard for me. Thankfully, he hadn't seemed to notice anything out of place, but the closer I approached, the groggier he looked.

He'd had trouble sleeping in the weeks since his father had taken his own life, and taking over Titan Transport had done a number on his mental health. The carefree kid I'd dated the last two summers had suddenly been replaced with a man that looked closer to forty than twenty. I felt a pang of guilt for adding to his anxiety with my dreams of growing the vineyard, but I was desperate for a hobby to keep my mind off of everything.

I reached the edge of the porch where he stood, steadying himself on the deck railing with his heavy palms as his eyes searched the water for me. "Hey there, I was just out for a walk, what are you doing up so late?"

His startled eyes focused on mine as I climbed the steps. "Hey, where did you come from?"

"Just around the corner. Are you okay?" I rested my hand on his shoulder like a good wife would.

"My eyes are so blurry I can hardly focus. Were you out swimming?"

I shook my head, pulling away from his touch quickly. "No. It was misting pretty heavily a few minutes ago."

"Oh." His grin tipped, lips finding mine. "I swear I haven't slept in so long I think I'm losing my mind." He dotted a kiss on my forehead. "You smell like a water baby."

My muscles tensed at his use of the term. He thought it innocent when my dad called me this particular nickname, but it was far from it. Only, it had happened so long ago I didn't even feel like the character at the center of that story, so explaining it to Morrissey had never seemed relevant.

"You know me, I love the smell of the beach." I shrugged, dancing away from his embrace, and clutched my journal to my chest, keeping it tucked neatly inside the blanket. If Morrissey ever found it, my life's secrets laid bare on the vanilla pages, he would never forgive me. Not because my sins were unforgivable, but because the illusion of his perfect life and legacy would be shattered in one swoop of ink.

Morrissey caught me at the waist and maneuvered my body toward his, one hand traveling to my hip and squeezing. "Come to bed."

"Okay," I managed, trying to keep the emotion from my voice. One of his hands began to slip under my coverup but I tensed, pushing his hand away. "Give me a minute first."

He tipped his head to one side, eyes chasing down my thighs and then back to my haunted face. "Are you sure you're okay?"

"Yes, I'm perfect." I pecked him on the lips. "Did you take something tonight? You seem pretty out of it, Mr. Sleepwalker."

Morrissey's eyes slithered down to my lips before he turned to head down the hallway to our master bedroom. "Only one pill, I could probably use another."

"Are you sure that wouldn't make things worse?" I paused at the bathroom doorway, concerned eyes on the back of my husband as he crawled into our bed.

"If I lose much more sleep, things will get a helluva lot worse at Titan. Damned if I do, damned if I don't, I guess."

I slipped around the corner as he spoke, sweeping my swimsuit off of my shoulders and throwing it under the bathroom sink to deal with later.

Maybe I would surprise him one of these days with my fabulous new skill, but today wasn't that day. With only the flowy chiffon coverup clothing my naked body, I climbed into bed, pressing my lips against his and getting lost in my husband.

The man I loved with all of my heart, even though I carried another man's baby.

CHAPTER TWENTY-SIX

Morrissey
Sixth day: 8.37 a.m.

My arms cut through the waves as I swam just offshore in the early morning. I'd been up wandering the halls all night, too afraid to go outside, too afraid to anchor myself to the pillow with sleeping pills, too afraid to . . . exist.

I was going nuts, and I'd begun to channel it in effective ways. I'd worked on the Titan Transport quarterly budgets for the following year, researched new winter hardy vines to introduce to the vineyard, and then I'd taken to opening one of the last remaining bottles of a vintage red blended in the wine barn.

My mind flashed back to the red-stained sheets still sitting on the table where Lenn had once practiced corking and sealing empty bottles in preparation for an upcoming harvest. A harvest that would probably never come.

I swam closer to the shore, feet digging into the sand as I retreated from the waves and jogged up the path to the house.

I reached the French doors, thankful for the two sleeping pills I'd knocked myself out with last night.

Tracking my sandy feet through the house, I peeled off my wet swim shorts and tossed them in the bathroom before wrapping a towel around my waist. I was just about to lock down the security system and jump in the shower when the loud buzzing alerted me to a visitor at the gate.

I groaned, moving to the kitchen to check the security cameras. I couldn't tell who it was, only a little white sports car waiting to be buzzed in. I squinted, hesitant to let anyone on the property at the moment. The memory of the few people gathered outside the press conference still made me cringe.

"Who is it?" I spoke into the speaker.

"Fawn, I've got something you need to see."

My heart raced, anxiety spiking in my body. I buzzed her in, an odd mix of regret and gratitude at her presence in my life again.

Fawn and I had dated in the months leading up to my first meeting with Lenn. She was working at the boat docks down by the marina one summer, and I was working valet at the yacht club next door. Once our paths crossed, there was no turning back for us — our click was loud and profound.

By the end of that summer, Fawn and I were over and Lenn and I were inseparable. Until now.

"Morning, Morrissey." Fawn air-kissed my cheek once I'd opened the front door. "Have you seen the newspaper?"

She thrust a rolled-up copy into my arms and nuzzled by me, then stood back to take me in — bare feet to tousled wet hair, only a towel in between.

"I've been avoiding it, actually."

"That's your first mistake. You're the man of the hour. Or week, should I say."

"What is Carl up to now?" I unfolded the news.

My stomach lurched.

I pushed away from the island, stumbling back outside into the fresh air. My eyes slammed closed before I screamed at the top of my lungs every curse word in my vocabulary.

"Did you get it all out?" Fawn was at my side, patting between my shoulder blades.

"I'm screwed, Fawn. Someone's already convinced I'm guilty and is working on everyone else in this town."

"Well, the headline says only accusations have been filed with the police — that's not proof of sexual misconduct."

"I didn't do it, didn't do anything."

"The girl that's come forward claims it happened while she was in high school, outside of a football game, in the parking lot. In *your* car."

"My car? I don't even go to high school football games, there can't be any proof of this."

"Proof or not, there's now an open investigation into your past, Morrissey. If there's anything at all I should know before we move forward, about this, or your wife, or anything that precedes that—"

"There's nothing, I have nothing, I know nothing, I did nothing. I don't know how to say it anymore. I don't know why this is happening to us."

She sighed, coming closer. Her touch was familiar, but not Lenn's. I'd grown so accustomed to Lenn's, even though our physical intimacy had faded after Tommy's birth, it wasn't out of lack of desire. "You have to be very careful now, no missteps."

"I hardly leave the Hollows, Fawn, it's become my own personal prison. That I'm mortgaged to the hilt on."

An empathetic smile crossed her lips. "I've missed your sense of humor."

I pushed my hand through my wet hair, thankful at least for the morning swim before this shitstorm cascaded down on me.

"I know you've been isolated out here on the Point, but going into town probably isn't the best idea right now. People are starting to . . . join teams. The Monroe family isn't exactly well-liked after the pensions at Titan went belly up."

I winced. I didn't blame them. "Teams?"

"About whether or not you—" she cleared her throat softly — "killed Lenn."

A headache suddenly pounded at the front of my brain. "There aren't enough sleeping pills in the world to deliver me from this hell, are there?"

"How long have you been on medication, Morrissey?"

"Since the business went under and my dad hung himself from the rafters of our pool house."

"It's been a rough few years for your family." She laced her fingers with mine, sadness in her eyes. "Just watch yourself, okay? With these new sexual misconduct allegations, well . . . from some perspectives it looks like you had a good reason to . . ." She paused, as if searching for the right words. "To find yourself not married anymore."

"Enough with the tiptoeing around, Fawn, I get it. The people in this town figure I found out about Carl and Lenn's affair and had my own, or worse, drowned my wife in a fit of rage."

Fawn didn't respond. I could see my words had startled her, but she didn't know what I knew. She hadn't read the journals after nearly shredding a man's hand in a grape crusher.

It had been a rough few nights.

"Thanks for hand-delivering the good news first thing in the morning." I pressed a hand at her back and walked her through the French doors and across the living room.

We'd just reached the front door when it swung wide, Kel filling the doorframe, a suspicious cut to his gaze. He eyed my nearly nude form, up and down, the towel clasped at my waist, and then Fawn, her sensible heels and pencil skirt accentuating a narrow waist and the kind of curves most men drool over.

Kel and I had drooled over Fawn through most of our early high school years, but we were different now — we all were.

"So, I assume you've seen the paper?"

"Got a good look first thing this morning, thanks to this one." I gestured to Fawn.

He raised an eyebrow, gaze lingering on the closeness of our shoulders, the presumed intimacy of us being here alone together.

"She's my lawyer."

Kel let the silence hang, mouth pursed tightly before he finally spoke. "You think it's the best idea hiring your ex as your lawyer?"

"It's not like that—"

"It doesn't matter what it is or isn't, it only matters how it looks — however any of this turns out, you'll be judged, Morrissey. It's in your best interest to take other people's perspectives to heart."

I hated his words, wanted to throw him out of the house before pounding his skull in with my fists. I'd never felt the kind of rage toward anyone that I felt in that moment toward Kel. Gone were the memories of football games and late nights partying at the sandbar. Now, he was only my nemesis, looking for clues to cement my guilt.

"What was I supposed to do, Kel? You keep showing up here implicating me in all this shit, it's like you've got your own personal propaganda network with Carl at the newspaper. Maybe I should launch my own investigation if I want any real answers."

"Well, I suppose it's good she's present for this then. Funny enough, I thought I'd catch you alone at this hour." His eyes narrowed on the towel at my waist. "The body that was found offshore of your boathouse a few nights ago was sent to the medical examiner. Toxicology came back clean. A six-inch gash that cracked the skull seems to be the cause of death. My guys were down by the shore late last night looking for anything we may have missed."

"And?" I breathed, wondering if that explained what I'd seen the night I'd found the journals. Maybe a reflection of flashlights or a play of the mist and moonlight.

"They found a broken bottle of your vintage — one bottled right here at the Hollows. It's cracked on the bottom and the lab just finished swabbing it. It's positive for blood."

"Oh my God."

"So, we've ordered ground penetrating radar from the main office. It should be here in a few hours and the tech crew will be out this afternoon to scan your property, vineyard included, for any anomalies or recent disturbances we may have missed."

Like a grave.

Acid burned in my stomach.

CHAPTER TWENTY-SEVEN

Lennox
Two summers ago — mid August

Secrets fester like wounds, truth pressing the lies out at every given angle.

"Hey, babe, why the sad face?" Morrissey wrapped his arms around my broken middle. I winced, avoiding our reflection in the mirror.

I thought I'd overcome the chill of violence that ran through me when I looked into his eyes, but with every passing week, the reminders grew. Maybe it was our newlywed status, the bills, or the fact that Morrissey had drawn early on his inheritance to buy us the house on Smokey Hollow Point for a wedding present.

He'd beamed with happiness when he'd shared a copy of the deed with me. I'd had to stop myself from breaking down in tears. What once was our dream now felt like my own personal nightmare. Everything about being in Thieves Cove reminded me of the things we'd lost. More and more I'd found myself wondering if he'd even questioned my absence that morning — why hadn't he come for me?

I pushed my feelings down, allowing Morrissey's hands to explore my waist. "Let's make a baby."

Dread cascaded through my system. "So soon? I still have college to finish and—"

"You could take online courses or finish at the community college maybe?"

"No, no. I told you I would marry you, but this fall I was going back to campus. I don't care about the big house or the Point, or—"

"I know, baby. I want what you want, remember?"

I pressed my lips together, wondering if that was really true. He'd been through so much since losing his dad in June, he'd refused to go back to U of M for his degree in the fall, choosing instead to help his mom with the business.

Instead of going back to campus, he'd gone to flight school. He was already running deliveries to the island as last pilot on staff at Titan Transport.

He'd single-handedly prevented the business from closing, but barely. He now ran the daily operations, and his mom took over the books for the company that his dad had run into the ground, nearly taking half of Thieves Cove down along with it.

My feelings toward the Monroe family had morphed in the time since I'd said yes. Then, my nightmare was still fresh, my brain unwilling to comprehend what it was that I was saying yes to, my only thought that this was the man I wanted to marry. That night in the pool house didn't change anything. Did it?

But sinking into Morrissey Monroe's arms now was harder than it had ever been. I'd taken his last name and picked up more shame. I lived in fear of my lies unraveling, and that I'd married a man with evil pulsing through his veins.

Morrissey had given me no indication that he meant me harm, but that didn't change that night or the trauma that radiated through me whenever his lips pressed my skin now. I recoiled at his touch, the idea of carrying his child growing more repulsive by the day.

I'd used Carl to reject my victimhood that night, allowed myself to fall into old memories, and in doing so, I'd prolonged the pain. Agonizing, self-annihilating pain. Regrets choked my throat every waking moment, the constant cloud suffocating on the occasions I was forced to interact with Carl since the night I'd lost myself in him.

"You and our family are the only things that matter to me. I spent so much time dodging my family name, but now that Dad is gone . . . all I want to do is honor him. He's the best man I've ever known, Lenn. His business and the family we create together is the only legacy he has and I want to make him proud."

My stomach churned.

The path was clear. I may not be going back to CMU for the fall semester, but I would need to make one last trip. My only backup option two hours away. I could be there and back while Morrissey was at work, I only had to hope he wouldn't find the evidence. I would need to be careful covering my tracks.

"Thank you for hanging in there with me." He interrupted my thoughts. "I know it wasn't easy watching my family crumble bit by bit, but you helped put us back together. You single-handedly put me back together. I know we can make magic, Lenn — with me flying now and this house and the vineyard, the sky's the limit."

"Winemaking, who would have thought?" I murmured, mind a million miles away. Could I even get an appointment at this late a date? "I'm going to take a walk."

"Want some company?" I had to resist stepping away from him, my focus elsewhere as I imagined taking care of this situation all on my own.

"No." I forced a smile. "I've been trying to read the manual for that industrial grape crusher in the back field. It's like a foreign language, I think my head might burst. I just need the sound of the waves for a few minutes to calm my mind."

"Perfect." He pecked me on the lips. "So damn perfect. This place, you, our lives. I love you, Lenn. I love you more than I knew was possible. I would have lost my mind without you by my side."

"Me too." I backed away, feeling the walls of the Hollows caving in. I slipped through the French doors and onto the wind-whipped wraparound, taking the steps barefoot before sinking into the damp seagrass.

I inhaled deeply, thankful when I turned to find him perched on the porch, a wave and a smile for me and only me. I waved back, turning my head before he could see the salty tears in my eyes as I thought about the appointment that would alter the course of my life forever.

How had I let my life get so out of control? And when had hiding become second nature to me?

By the time I was over the sandy knoll and had reached the water's edge, I dropped to my knees and vomited into the bubbling water. The round rocks, worn smooth with time, pinched my knees as I scooped up the April water with my hands and splashed my face. The water mixed with my tears as my mind cycled back to Mick Jagger bellowing in my ear, the force of a stranger's body tearing my own.

"I hate everything," I sobbed, wishing I could gouge the memories from my mind like a surgeon with a scalpel.

They tormented me, these thoughts of mine.

I wondered if this was what womanhood was like for my mother, cruel and vicious, or if her experience would be my own. Did cycles repeat? Was I destined to fail as epically as she had? I crawled deeper into the waves, letting the water lap at my thighs and elbows, before my fingertips loosened and water flowed freely.

Instead of the white-hot terror that soaked my bones when I normally came close to the bay, a serene sense of ease permeated me to the marrow. I measured my breaths, steady and slow, before flipping onto my back and stretching my gaze to the clouds.

So dark, so ominous, so beautiful.

The roar of the underwater current rushed in my ears, gulls swirling above my head, before I let my eyes fall closed and released myself. Untethered, I floated. The waves pulled me out, the current carried me back in. I imagined the calm that would follow if I let my lungs vacate their last breaths and I slipped under.

Ever so quietly.

The water was too cold to allow me to feel, the pain melting to numbness. How easy to slip quietly under the surf like Ophelia, a water baby succumbing to its simplest form.

Death: my soul's only prescription.

CHAPTER TWENTY-EIGHT

Morrissey
Sixth day: 2.17 p.m.

"I appreciate your patience while we figure this out." Kel grinned sheepishly at me. He stood with one shoulder propped against the wine barn, the tech crew finally finishing up the last third of the vineyard scan with the ground penetrating radar. No one had to explain to me what they were looking for; they were searching for a disturbance in the dirt or anything unnatural underground that would indicate a recently dug grave.

They'd paid extra attention to the area around the grape crusher, especially the zone where I'd dug up the journals, but so far, they didn't seem alerted to any unnatural disturbances in the dirt.

"Did I have a choice?" I answered Kel as I moved away from the barn with my hands in my pockets.

"You know we go way back. I'm just here to help you, and maybe you can help me."

"Whatever I can do."

"Do you keep an inventory of the bottles that come and go through the Hollows?"

"I don't even know, that's all Lenn's job, she filled me in on some of the vineyard stuff, but I've been so wrapped up with Titan I didn't even catch everything she said about it over the months."

"Well, so far this is an open investigation, and I'm trying to look at this with clear eyes, but with all the happenings up here on the Point over the last week, I don't think anyone in Thieves Cove knows what to make of it."

"Seems logical that I'd be accused of an assault that didn't happen then too, right?"

"Morrissey, I'm not saying that, it's just . . . I'm doing my best to keep an eye on things."

"Well, thanks for the warning. Can you tell me at least who the girl is that's accusing me of whatever at the football game?"

Kel paused, eyes hanging on mine. Sorrow laced the irises I'd known since childhood. "You know I can't reveal that."

Bile burned at the base of my throat. I was at a loss, a complete and utter loss, how best to approach this — I was sick to death of just letting this string of tragedies happen to me. "Perfect."

I walked off toward the house.

"Morrissey—" Kel paused, conflict in his eyes — "that body in the bay, it's the accuser's brother."

My shoulders stiffened, freight trains pounding in my ears. "What's his name?"

"It's Spalding Thurston — your realtor's son."

CHAPTER TWENTY-NINE

Morrissey
Sixth night: 7.22 p.m.

Macy Thurston had sold us the Hollows.

Macy had been at the press conference. I vaguely remembered her offering up the use of her son anytime to help around the vineyard if I needed it. I was pretty sure Kel had witnessed her offer.

And now Spalding was dead.

I held my hands over my face, leaning over the stack of journals as the sun sank in the sky later that evening. This looked bad — like I was guilty of whatever Spalding's sister had accused me of, that he'd discovered something incriminating and confronted me . . . and now he was dead.

I was now on a mission, determined to find the answers in the last few remaining journals that I hadn't read the night before last. Whoever had ripped the pages from them had been trying to hide something, or reveal it, I wasn't sure.

And what did the lake have to do with anything? Why would Lenn spend time there when she usually avoided it at all costs?

Maybe if it were daytime, I could be convinced that they'd just gone for a boat ride in the bay and suffered a tragic accident where she'd saved my son just as a wave took her under, but . . . the hat, the water, the boathouse, the security footage, none of it made sense.

Coupled with the newspaper articles that had been printed the last few days, the only thing that did make sense was . . . *me.*

Maybe the sleeping pills were wreaking more havoc than I realized. I pulled out my phone, running a quick internet search on the prescription I was on in addition to sleepwalking. Millions of hits came up, and it didn't take me long to scroll to a headline that piqued my interest.

I spent exactly three minutes reading a personal blog post about a night with sleeping pills gone horribly wrong, and I closed the browser altogether.

I was sure if I'd done something as horrible as hurting my family while I was sleepwalking, there would be more evidence of it, right?

Blood on my hands . . .

And then my eyes fell on the stacks of journals and bloody sheets spread out in front of me.

"Shit."

This didn't look good at all. If Kel found these and that blood was in fact Lenn's . . . well, it only implicated me in her disappearance more than I already had been.

Public opinion would not be in my favor on this one. I had half a mind to re-bury the sheets and journals, then wondered, if I'd never dug them up to begin with, whether Kel and his team would have found them today.

I didn't know much about the laser scanning technology they were using, only that technicians would be poring over the findings in the coming days and then reporting back to Kel.

I stood up from the table, flicking off the light in the wine barn and making sure this time to lock the barn door behind me with the padlock. Kel had been standing against this door just hours ago, incriminating evidence right behind his back that I hadn't even thought to hide.

By the time I was in the kitchen of the silent house, my hands were wrapped around the neck of a vodka bottle. I avoided the sleeping pills, taking a shot to shake off the edge this day had left me with. I sat at the kitchen island, the newspaper from earlier laid bare on the dark granite.

I sighed, taking another shot and scanning the article.

It was a nothing burger through and through, and Carl was grasping at straws, whatever he was up to. I just couldn't figure out what kind of high schooler would accuse me of something this disgusting. It had to be a case of mistaken identity . . . unless . . . unless it was another example of one of my unfortunate run-ins with sleeping pills.

I took another shot, unwilling to even consider it.

People can tell when evil lives inside them. I had to believe that. But then, what did that say about Lenn's lies and her affair with Carl? Did I think she was evil for breaking up our family? Maybe. Would it end up being a blessing in disguise? The jury was still out.

I slammed another shot back, then stood from my chair, feeling like I had to get to the bottom of this before I was implicated in a whole slew of shit I had no recollection of doing.

I walked out the front door, eyes on the starry sky. It was warm, so I pulled out one of the bicycles left by the previous owners and set off down the driveway and over the knoll. I slipped through the gap in the gate, then took off down Smokey Hollow Road, the wind on my face the first real sense of freedom I'd had since this all started.

It didn't take me long to wind my way down the road, every turn bringing me closer and closer to downtown. Navigating the road was dangerous, and the night Kel had had his accident on the bluff with the tourist girl came back as I cycled past the barrier that looked over the steep edge.

A cool wind sent a chill up my spine as I crested the edge and then began speeding downhill. Shadows from the towering evergreens on one side danced and played tricks with my mind, like a lurking stranger in the night. I hadn't checked the clock when I'd gone off on my ride, but considering I was nearing the final turn into town, I had to have been gone for at least thirty minutes.

I slowed, turning quietly into a residential area lit with yellow street lamps. Signs littered the front yards like political ads, and it wasn't until I cycled closer that I saw what they advertised: my arrest.

A pit of dread settled in my stomach as I pedaled faster, some of the handwritten signs demanding my arrest for the murder of my wife, others reminding fellow citizens of the "innocent until proven guilty" perspective on criminal justice.

Fawn's warning earlier about staying out of town now rang loud and clear.

I was about to whip my bike around and head right back up Smokey Hollow when I spied the light still on at the newspaper office, Carl's tiny gray Honda parked out front. Without thinking, I pedaled across the street, slipping into the shadows and leaving my bike at the edge of the brick wall.

I slipped along the building, clinging to the darkness, knowing that Kel could pull this security footage tomorrow and then where would I be? I just wanted to have a little chat with Carl anyway, clearly he had it out for me.

I tapped on the windowpane, almost surprised when his lanky form came around the hallway and opened the door. He stuck his head out. "Hello?"

"We need to chat, Carl."

His eyebrows rose. "Monroe?"

I nearly snarled in reply. "Is that any way to greet your best friend's husband?" I slipped in the crack, pushing him back against the painted cement brick wall.

"Hey, I don't want trouble."

"What do you want, Carl?" I was seething, the vodka worn off in my bloodstream, replaced by vicious adrenaline.

"The truth. I want the truth."

"The truth?" I fumed. "It doesn't look like that from here. I know you and Lenn had a thing back then. You redacted your name, but you think I don't know my wife?"

"Do you?" He raged. "Do you!"

"When did your affair start up again? Or did you take her because she denied you?"

Carl smashed his squared fist into my lip. I tasted the blood instantly.

"You've got it wrong, Morrissey. From the beginning you've always gotten it wrong, especially with Lennox."

"What do you know?" I raged, wrapping my hand around his windpipe and pressing. "What did you do? Why were you fighting with my wife the night she disappeared?"

"I've already discussed this with Kel."

Anger zapped through me before I pushed away from him and crossed the room. I flung stacks of boxes, whipped trays of papers, opened file cabinets. "Where's the rest?"

"The rest of what?"

"Whatever you're going to print tomorrow to slander me, where is it? What more do you have and who are you getting it from?"

Carl lingered, arms crossed as he watched me come undone. "Where *did* I get it, Morrissey?"

I clamped down on my teeth, feeling like this was all some elaborate verbal ruse to send me over the edge of sanity.

"What game are you playing?"

"What game are you? Didn't you ever ask yourself where Lenn went that night? Not Lenn your wife, Lenn the girl we both loved."

"Loved?" I snarled, feeling my blood return to boiling. "She didn't love you, she loathed you. If you'd seen the rest of those journals, you'd realize she couldn't hate anyone more. Your pathetic advances drove her away."

Carl's lips turned up, a visceral growl escaping his chest before he charged me in the newsroom, sending us flying over a desk. The screech filled my ears as we crashed into the cement wall in the corner, my head hitting the bricks and stars flooding my vision.

"You seem stressed, Morrissey. Getting much sleep lately?" His words were haunting, the restless nights compounding in one fell swoop.

"You try watching the police scan your backyard for the body of your wife and talk to me about stress. Every breath feels like walking on eggshells. The next time Kel comes to the Point it'll be to arrest me."

"They won't find her there, will they, Monroe? You know where she is, don't you? Where are you keeping her, you sick son of a bitch!"

"You're nuts." I pushed him off of me, limping my way to the door.

"We're gonna find her, Morrissey Monroe, we're gonna find her and then we're gonna nail your ass to the cross for everything you did to her for all those years. And then, I'm gonna get my son back."

CHAPTER THIRTY

Lennox
Two summers ago — late August

"Oh my God."

Our pristine organic cotton sheets were soiled with a wide bloodstain.

"Are you okay, babe?" Morrissey popped his head into the doorway.

"Yeah, I just started my period." I ripped the sheets forcefully, gathering them in my arms so he wouldn't see the evidence of my deception.

I loved him, but my love was tainted. I'd loved him with lies.

"You want me to throw those in the wash before I leave for work?"

"No thanks." I was facing away, tears already streaming as I realized what must be happening.

The baby. The pregnancy. Vanished.

"'Kay. I should be back for lunch around noon. Have a great morning. Love you."

I waited for his familiar embrace and peck on the forehead, but it didn't come. I breathed a sigh of relief, collapsing into the bundle of sheets when I heard the front door slam behind him. I gasped loudly, my pain too loud to control now as tiny twists in my stomach grew to a dull ache.

I was miscarrying a baby that didn't even feel like mine.

I stumbled to standing, unwilling to succumb to the pain before the cramp in my stomach turned deadly. I leaned against the wall, new waves of warmth coating my inner thighs. I glanced between my feet, the white sheets coated in fresh crimson stains.

"No." I cried new tears, devastation taking its toll on my body.

Maybe this was a sign — the miscarriage was karma for a baby I didn't know how to love.

"I'm so sorry, baby." I cradled my stomach, rocking softly as if I were holding its newborn warmth in my arms. I hummed softly as the wetness on my cheeks turned to stains and the ache in my belly faded.

I gulped down my grief, unsteady as I pushed myself up. I stumbled into our bathroom, climbing into the tub and letting the hot water roll over my cold body. I looked like a fighter fresh out of the ring, red swirls painting the drain and carrying away a life.

By the time the water ran cold, I turned it off and climbed out, wrapping myself in Morrissey's fluffy oversized robe and returning to the sheets. I'd never be able to get the stains out of the sheets, and I didn't want to. This was the only evidence that my child had existed, if only for a few short moments.

I thought of the chest that contained the stacks of my moleskin journals. I'd begun to fill them obsessively in the weeks leading up to this, the only friend I could trust those blank pages. I made my way to the back of our walk-in closet, digging past moving boxes that we still hadn't unpacked, behind my wedding dress, the intricate beads and lace I'd purchased off the rack belying the shame that had burned beneath.

My fingertips landed on the worn wood of the chest my dad had made me when I was a baby. Beneath the hand-knit blanket from my grandmother, I found the remaining stack of my journals, gathering them all in the center of the stained sheets and then wrapping them in a tight bundle. I tied them until they were no bigger than the size of a newborn and then pushed Morrissey's robe off of my shoulders and fumbled for the nearest casual dress within reach.

I slipped it on, then gathered the bundle in my arms and walked out of the French doors in our bedroom, down the wraparound porch steps and across the yard to the wine barn. I unhooked it quickly, eyes scanning the hundreds of trellises of grape vines beyond. We were all alone out here, and I'd never been so grateful.

My hand locked around a small garden spade, and with the bundle under my arm, I hustled to the farthest corner of the vineyard. I paused, eyes on the grape crusher as I looked for an area that, if disturbed, wouldn't stand out. A patch of gravel spread off the back edge, so I dropped the sheets in the damp grass and began digging.

I dug and dug, deeper and deeper, until my knuckles ached and sweat beaded my brow. When I figured it was deep enough that it would go unnoticed for an eternity, I dropped to my knees and gathered the bundle of sheets, and my words, in my arms. A permanent ache settled in a corner of my heart as I placed a soft kiss to the sheets, emotion hovering behind my lids as I put it into the ground without any pomp or circumstance.

My first child, buried in a shallow grave in my backyard.

I splayed my palms over the bundle, tears drifting down the angles of my face as I breathed a small prayer for the little angel that didn't ask to come into this world — and didn't ask to be snatched out of it. Both of us a victim of our circumstances.

"I love you, little one. I hope you can forgive me someday."

And with that, I pushed layers of dark dirt over the crisp sheets, burying my past in the name of my future.

CHAPTER THIRTY-ONE

Morrissey
Sixth night: 10.00 p.m.

Carl's words echoed in my mind.

I'm gonna get my son back.

Was Tommy his?

Had I been played for a fool from the start, Lenn only after status, and Carl her real love?

I couldn't bear the thought, all the sweet moments that had once filled my memories of our relationship now replaced by all the moments she'd been impressed with the things I'd given her, or the life I'd wanted to breathe into us someday. And I'd fallen right into her trap. Buying the Hollows for her like a lovesick chump.

My mother's warning when I told her I wanted to pull out my inheritance to buy Lenn the house rang loud and clear; the fact that I'd emptied the remainder of my account for the down payment on this house as a wedding gift had nearly exploded Gigi's mind.

And now it was no wonder.

Maybe Lenn had only been concerned about my legacy in as far as it would cement her place in my world.

I hated thinking that way, but the world Lenn came from wasn't pretty. I'd always known she carried darkness in her past, I'd just thought that's where it belonged and would stay. Never could it affect our simple life.

How very wrong I'd been.

Had Lenn lied to Carl about the miscarriage? Told him she'd had one when she hadn't — but then, how could that explain the bloody sheets? Unless this elaborate ruse had all been created for me in the first place.

I still couldn't wrap my brain around the possibilities, and I didn't even want to. Just days ago, my biggest problem had been balancing the books at Titan, now it was whether to hire a second lawyer to represent me in a possible homicide case.

The questions still lingering in my mind when I finished the last entry on the final moleskin journal: Had the miscarriage really happened? Had Lenn and Carl's affair continued after our wedding? What did Carl really know, and what did Carl only *think* he knew?

I lingered at the front window of the Hollows, letting my eyes unfocus as the lighthouse beam looped in forever circles.

Something caught my eye then. I squinted through the low-hanging mist, quietly opening the French doors and closing them quickly before the house alarm went off. Hunkered low in the shadows, I crept along the knoll before turning down the path that led along the rocky shoreline. I picked my way slowly in the direction of the boathouse, thinking how the figure looked eerily like the hunched goat farmer rowing a skiff in the distance.

I blinked quickly, looking around to see if I was truly alone, the feeling of someone's eyes now always prickling the back of my neck. There'd been so many coincidences over the last few days, it was impossible not to consider I was being watched.

The figure in the skiff rowed with more haste, hunching lower as the boat grew tinier and tinier.

What had I just seen? Had it all been a figment of my imagination? Or was someone really creeping around my house — a stranger, or someone I knew all too well?

A shiver coursed down my spine as I moved along the rocks, sidling up against the shingled cedar wall of the boathouse. I sucked in a damp breath, forcing the happy memories from my mind at this spot, and lifting myself up over the deck railing. I punched in the security code and let myself in. I didn't dare flick on a light, but Kel and his team had already worked their way up and down this space, so I didn't expect to find anything anyway.

But why was I here?

I wasn't sure.

I stumbled along the wooden deck boards, aural senses on high alert as the gentle lapping beneath the boathouse set my teeth on edge. It was too peaceful, too still, like the calm before the storm. I picked my way along the wicker furniture that dotted the space, eyes assessing the boat that sat anchored most days of the year.

I opened the supply closet, the gentle hum of the generator loudening as a beam of moonlight lit the polished oak. A handheld grape masher lay on the floor, dried specks of what looked like blood decorating the heavy iron end. So out of place in an otherwise perfectly pristine space.

It was heavy, and the tiny barbs on the business end added extra force when used like a mortar and pestle on small batches of grapes. The design was old, a vintage winemaking item Lenn had tracked down last summer.

I bent, grasping the worn wooden handle and bringing it into the light. The faint tinge of copper filled my nostrils.

I gulped, thinking this wasn't what it seemed like, before tucking the handheld masher in the back pocket of my jeans and walking back out of the boathouse as quietly as I'd come.

I tried not to let it register that I may have just found the weapon that had murdered my wife and son.

How could investigators have missed this? And what else had they overlooked?

CHAPTER THIRTY-TWO

Morrissey
Seventh day: 7.52 a.m.

I tapped the head of the grape masher in my hand as I approached the house.

Cresting the knoll, I stopped dead in my tracks.

A white sports car sat at the gate, a long pair of legs crossed at the ankles as the driver watched me approach.

"Fawn. Lovely to see you." Sarcasm rippled my words; I didn't care if she picked up on it.

"We need to discuss some things in the case. Can't wait."

I punched the security code into the gate box and it slid open. She got behind the wheel of her car and entered, the gate closing behind her as she crawled up my driveway with her window rolled down.

"I've got a low-level informant in the police force that says Kel is in possession of a CCTV video that shows you lurking that night near the boathouse, only minutes after Lenn and Tommy are on camera."

"Minutes? How can that be?" I blinked rapidly, none of it making sense. "Why didn't Kel tell me they have footage of Lenn and Tommy that night?"

"Apparently it's grainy, out of focus, and there's something else . . ." Her car pulled to a slow stop, and she cut the engine and unfolded herself from behind the wheel. "It doesn't show what happened, only shows that they were there around that time — a dash of yellow in the top of the screen and then it's blank again. Next thing you know, you come through the next morning and find the hat floating in the water. That's very clear."

"Have you seen this video?" I asked.

She didn't answer, eyes averting. "I used to date a guy on the force, he sent me the file."

"Let me see it," I bit.

She shook her head. "I can't do that."

"What do you mean, you can't? You're my lawyer, where's my client privilege now?" I grasped her elbow, pulling her to me and hissing at her ear, "Show me that video or get the hell out of my house."

Her eyes flashed with anger, muscles stiffening under my grip before she threw me off, snarling as she backed away and then dug through her bag. "Here."

I took the phone from her, the video already playing.

It was dark, the normally grainy video made grainier by the fog rolling off the bay and lingering around the edges of the boathouse. I could make out the peaked roof though, and the worn dock in the foreground.

I couldn't believe I was scrutinizing footage in search of an answer about a kidnapping.

"See it?" She was at my ear again.

Just as she said the words, I could see the flash of yellow she'd spoken of — there for only an instant before it was gone again.

"It looks like someone was running down the dock with him."

"Exactly. Lennox comes next."

She did then, her gait frantic as she ran to the edge of the frame and then out of view.

"That's it."

"There's nothing else? Nobody else? Just the two of them?"

"Well, almost."

"Almost?" I was almost afraid of her reply.

"There's debate on the force about the few seconds before, if someone is waiting out of sight, watching them."

"Watching them?" Fear welled inside of me at the thought that this had all been premeditated. My family unsafe, right under my own eyes.

"There's movement in the trees beyond the boathouse, a shadow slips back into the treeline, but some of the guys say it's just the moon reflecting off the windows. Kel and some of the others though . . . they're more suspicious."

"Do they think someone tried to kidnap Tommy, and Lenn chased after them?"

She nodded, eyes hovering on mine before she finally answered: "You."

CHAPTER THIRTY-THREE

Morrissey
Seventh day: 8.32 a.m.

"I can't believe this is my life." I uttered the only thing running through my mind.

"That's not very helpful," Fawn said.

"Play it again." I zoomed in on the scene where the shadow came into the picture. "It looks edited."

"Edited?" She scrunched her eyebrows in dismay.

"I think this is fake. All of it. I don't even know if that's really Tommy."

"You really think it's fake?" Her face was incredulous.

I shrugged, feeling bold. I flung the masher out on the kitchen island and it skidded to a halt just at the edge of the counter.

"Holy shit, Morrissey, did you murder your wife?"

I huffed. "Just wait." I sped down the hallway, swiping one of the journals I'd brought into the house and left at my bedside table. "Read this."

I flung it sideways and it landed splayed open, Lenn's fevered chicken scratch filling the pages.

"And these." I threw the bundle of bloody sheets onto the counter.

Horror crossed her measured features.

"What are you saying here?" She moved closer to the sheets.

"I don't know," I answered. "I really don't know."

"That's not a good answer."

I rested my head in both of my hands, elbows on the cold granite. "I'm just waiting for Kel to waltz in here and arrest me."

"I'm suddenly rethinking offering my counsel."

"I don't blame you."

"Morrissey." She rocked against my shoulder like we were best buds again. "I'm kidding, geez. We've known each other since middle school, I don't really think you're a murderer. And even if you are, we could probably settle with big pharma about that little sleeping pill addiction you've got. We can make it work."

"Lovely, Fawn. Maybe I should just turn myself in now."

"And say what?"

I shrugged, hands fisting at the sheets. "Why does the only other good option feel like drinking the rest of that bottle of vodka and walking into Lake Michigan?"

"Oh, don't be dramatic, Monroe. It doesn't suit you."

I laughed out loud, something closer to maniacal than light-hearted.

"So—" she settled at the barstool next to me — "where did you find these?"

"The sheets and a few dozen journals were buried by the grape crusher." I fingered the edge of the fitted sheet. "And the masher I found right before you showed up."

"Convenient." Her eyes gleamed with mystery. I could almost hear her brain working. "Was the masher with the sheets?"

"No, at the boathouse."

"Where the security footage shows all of you that night?"

"Not *all* of us."

"Right. Your wife, your son, and a phantom."

I scowled, resenting her bold truthfulness. “Or the goat farmer.”

“Are you kidding?”

I shrugged. “He’s got motive, opportunity, access — what more does he need?”

She pondered my words silently, eyes cast to the dark bay out of the picture windows. The lighthouse flashed ominously, barely cutting through the oppressive drizzle that lingered around the Point this time of year.

She slid out another file with hundreds of loose sheets stacked inside. “Now that that’s out of the way, I’ve been doing some research.”

“I guess so,” I breathed, sifting through the top few papers. Copies of newspaper articles about Titan Transport closing and the missing pensions and a group threatening to bring legal action against my father’s estate.

“A lot of people in this town have it out for your family.”

I groaned. I’d been in a bubble as a kid. My father never talked about business when he was at home, and he wasn’t home much. “I guess I didn’t realize the impact Titan had on this town.”

“Your father came in and saved the town when he decided to expand Titan two decades ago. My father was the head mechanic at the big shop for a few years. I think they had a falling out though — either with management or your dad, he never said. I didn’t think about it much until I spotted an ad in the newspaper a few weeks ago about a meeting for former employees of Titan.”

“A meeting? About my company?”

“Is it really your company, Morrissey? It supported the economy of an entire town. It became the people’s company at that point.”

“Well, they aren’t the ones suffocating under the bills,” I grumbled.

“Or living on the Point.”

I huffed. “I didn’t know.”

"It sounds like there are a lot of things you didn't know."

I let her words hang, hating that they rang so true. "This conversation is giving me a headache."

She didn't say a word, only slipped her hands along the ridges of my shoulders and then started to rub. Her fingertips worked magic at the base of my neck, loosening the muscles and making me feel a little more human for the first time in days.

"I can't imagine what this must be like for you," she purred, running her palms down my back and pressing at different pressure points. It felt good to have her hands on me — too good. "You're still the best man I've ever known, Monroe. I've dated a lot of losers since you broke up with me, and none of them hold a candle."

I didn't answer, unsure of the right thing to say at that moment.

I felt her breath as she neared; the brush of her lips at the skin of my neck sent a shiver coursing through me. She felt too familiar, like it would be too easy to fall into the escape she offered.

"Fawn, what we had before . . ." I cleared my throat, feeling my body's stubborn reaction to her despite the time that had gone by. "We can't keep doing this. Not now. Not *again*."

She moved to the edge of my lips, brushing me with the softest of kisses before she moved away, leaving space between us wider than the bay outside the picture windows. "I can't stop thinking that you would be mine right now, if . . . if . . ."

She sniffed, dabbing at her eyes. She was so pretty, the look in her eyes so warm, it made me wish for simpler times, when kissing Fawn felt natural, before I was flooded with terror at the thought of Lenn and Tommy missing.

"I can leave this with you if you'd like." She gestured to the stacks of printouts. "I highlighted some spots I had questions about though, maybe you can answer some of them. I want to help you find them, and to keep your ass out of jail, Morrissey. Despite everything that happened between us, I want that for you."

"Can we go through it right now? I can make a pot of coffee and we can work through the day on this. I think it's about time Kel called the state in — he's got a lot on his plate, and I don't know if he's got the time or manpower to find her."

"You're suggesting we do?"

"I think we've got a helluva lot more to work with than he does."

She sank down into the leather couch, a frown crossing her features. "You're going to have to turn over that grape masher to the forensic team, Morrissey."

A trickle of fear swam through me.

"I know, Fawn, I just don't know if I'm ready for what they might find."

"Exactly why I don't want Kel to call the state in — you'd probably find yourself booked in tonight for withholding evidence in a murder investigation. Would you be willing to let me see the journals you found?"

I paused, figuring the stack I'd brought into the house were the tame ones. The journal that detailed the moments surrounding the night she and Carl were together I'd wrapped in a strip of burlap and hidden behind the work table in the wine barn. "You can flip through this one—" I indicated the one I'd brought into the kitchen — "I've just got to check on something for a minute."

One of Fawn's eyebrows rose in curiosity before she shrugged and plucked the journal off of the counter.

I didn't say anything else, only escaped down the hallway and through the doors in our bedroom. I picked my way through the silence of our backyard before reaching the dark wine barn. I unlocked the door with the key I'd begun carrying with me everywhere and left the light off, only following the silver moonbeams as I crept across the small workspace. I slipped a hand behind the small floor cooler where the last remaining bottles of the Hollows vintage red were stored.

I kneeled, growling when I couldn't locate the journal I'd tucked behind here just yesterday. I gripped the edge, reaching further behind the cooler, when something punctured my palm. I yelped, bringing my hand to the light to find a small gash at the base that trickled crimson.

"What was that?" I whispered to myself, inspecting the cooler to find a jagged gash where the glass door had been broken open. A hole larger than a fist gaped near the top corner, large enough for a bottle of wine to be passed through.

I pushed the wine cooler back from the wall without even realizing I was leaving my fingerprints all over the thing, before clamping onto the journal that had brought me in here. I unwrapped the burlap, wrapping it instead around my bleeding hand before tucking the journal under my arm and backing out of the barn.

"There you are."

My body went rigid.

"It's just me." Fawn's palms were at my elbows. "What happened?"

I shook my head. "The door on the cooler is broken, I cut my hand."

"Hm, you've got quite the strange look on your face, like you've seen a ghost." She took my hand in hers. "Let's get you cleaned up."

"Yeah," I breathed, letting her lead me out, puzzling over who had broken into the wine cooler right under my nose and why the missing bottle had turned up near Spalding Thurston's dead body in the bay.

CHAPTER THIRTY-FOUR

Lennox
Six days ago

I know you lied about the miscarriage.

A shiver ran through me as I swiped right on my phone to delete Carl's message.

GOLD DIGGER.

I WANT A PATERNITY TEST.

Fear rattled my bones.

No. Please, Carl, I've told you: Tommy is a Monroe.

I waited impatiently, wondering if talking to him was wrong or right.

LET ME SPEND TIME WITH HIM. I SHOULD KNOW MY OWN SON.

My fingers trembled as I imagined what that would mean. Would twenty minutes be enough to convince him Tommy was a Monroe? And could I really orchestrate a way for them to be together without Morrissey knowing?

I shook my head, realizing how crazy it was since Tommy *was* a Monroe. In blood and name. We'd learned Halloween morning that I was expecting and quiet tears had filled

Morrissey's eyes when I'd revealed the news to him. Tommy had arrived in this world our precious preemie baby, my pregnancy with him a tough one, maybe made worse by the scar tissue from my first miscarriage. Tommy, born eleven weeks ahead of schedule this past April, was our miracle baby. It had taken me months to shake the feeling that we might lose our newborn infant while he breathed with the help of a machine in the neonatal intensive care unit.

Fire tore through my veins as I remembered the tearful nights Morrissey and I had endured as we prayed our son would survive and someday thrive against all odds. We'd taken all-night shifts and slept in hard chairs in the waiting room so he would never be alone. Coming through that emotional hardship together had healed the scars surrounding our marriage in so many ways and made the gift of Tommy's life more priceless than I could express.

No, Carl, he isn't yours to know. I'm sorry, I want the best for you, but it's not healthy for me to talk to you anymore.

HEALTHY FOR YOU? YOU RUINED MY LIFE. YOU STOLE MY SON. IF YOU DON'T LET ME GET TO KNOW HIM I'LL MAKE YOU REGRET ALL OF THE PAIN YOU'VE MADE ME SUFFER ALL OF THESE YEARS.

Tears bloomed at the corners of my eyes as I sat at my office desk, the video monitor showing me my five-month-old little boy sleeping soundly in the nursery next door.

I HAVE RIGHTS, BITCH.

I jumped at the uncharacteristic nastiness in Carl's words. I didn't know this man he'd become.

I glanced at the stack of bills that sat unpaid next to the keyboard, heart in my throat as I fingered the edge of one from Fawn Fitzgerald, attorney-at-law. I didn't have the money to pay three hundred an hour, but somehow I'd sensed this day with Carl coming. His erratic behavior had degenerated over the last year and I hadn't been able to sleep through the night since Tommy was born, haunted by the irrational sense that he might be taken from me, or worse, that I might do something to put him in harm's way.

Fawn was a year older than me. We first met when I was twelve and we rode the school bus together. I thought she was cool because she smoked cigarettes and talked about kissing boys. What I'd really envied was the way she carried herself like she didn't care what anyone thought, and she still didn't. It made her ruthless in the courtroom and she and I became fast friends when she'd been assigned the property law case at the Hollows.

A few coffee dates turned into margarita happy hours, and I found myself revealing all of my secrets, including what happened on the worst night of my life. I'd sworn her to an oath of tequila-induced sisterhood, and then told her a little about Carl and how he was convinced Tommy was his. She'd leaned in close, waved a hand and then told me she could have papers printed in a jiff that would prove paternity in favor of Morrissey.

She'd delivered on her word.

The following morning a sealed envelope had arrived by courier at the Hollows: contained within, undeniable proof that Tommy was a Monroe, right down to his DNA.

Fawn was a godsend, now I had only to deliver the papers to Carl.

I'd already told Morrissey I had a design mockup and copy for Pumpkin Fest to deliver before morning, but the prospect of seeing Carl now left me on edge and regretting my plan altogether.

DON'T MAKE ME GET A LAWYER.

Fingers shaking, I typed: *I have proof. Meet me at the newspaper tonight at 9.*

I nearly fainted as the three little dots blinked across the screen.

OKAY.

I set my phone down, pushing away from my desk and hugging myself as I paced the room.

There was so much raining down on me, but the only thing that really mattered was the sweet little boy sleeping across the hallway. Securing his future was my only concern.

But how secure could it be if I couldn't get the two-million-dollar property to make money for us?

How bright was our future when I'd already hired a lawyer to kick the neighbor off of his property?

I glanced again at the bill from Fawn, the three thousand dollars taunting me before I snatched the invoice and ran down the hallway, pushing through the French doors and running out into the cool autumn air.

Feet slipping through the damp grass, I passed the barn and ran down a row of dead grape vines, tears running faster and mixing with the drizzle. I didn't stop when I came to the grape crusher, only running faster as I crested the knoll and then nearly slid down the overgrown edge.

I halted just short of the ramble of barbed wire and rotten posts that did little to keep the goats in. They bleated now, the sound echoing relentlessly, the crying of dozens and dozens of the furry beasts descending on my ears, surrounding me in a brain fog. They cut through my last ragged nerve and caused my own frustrated scream to erupt from my lungs as I held the fence down and hopped over the tangled barbs.

I ran then, the soft grass turning to rocky mud as I headed for the looming shadow of the goat shed.

The noise grew louder. A group of the tallest goats had gathered at a gate, hooves on the half-door, cries erupting from their mouths.

"What is going on?" I cried when I saw a spray of blood land in the mud near the gate. Another splatter of crimson on the light pole. Another cry. More red. My tears burned with salt as I rushed misty-eyed around the corner to find the source of the gory murder.

"What are you doing?!"

He didn't hear me, the goats chorusing loudly over my own croaked voice.

Something else caught his attention then, and he halted his action, looming around to face me fully. The goat farmer's white butcher's jacket was painted a violent shade of red. He held a machete in one hand, a sacrificed kid hanging upside down over his shoulder.

The mother goats bleated.

My heart sank.

"What are you doing?"

With gravel in his voice, he mumbled, "Coyotes got ahold of him so I put him out of his misery, I'm saving what salvageable meat there is before it spoils. What are you doing on my property?"

My hands trembled as the mother goat fixed her large marble eyes on me.

"I . . . Do you have to do that with them here?"

"They don't know."

"They can sense it." My voice trembled. "And smell."

His eyes darkened. "Why are you here? To insult me?"

I squared my shoulders. "You can't contain them."

"Been contained the last week. Kept 'em in the barn, I'll do it 'til I can replace the fence separating our property lines if that's what it takes to keep your fancy bullshit lawyer off my land." His eyes cast down to my feet, my house slippers covered in mud. "And you."

I couldn't walk away, not now, not after everything. My problems were his fault, my lost harvest and the mounting bills. It was all too much.

"I want you to pay for some of the hours my lawyer put in for researching the property laws. She also had to hire a land surveyor to count off the feet of the easement; she's itemized that right here." I pointed to the damp paper clinging to my palm.

"I don't give a shit about your lawyer. She didn't find out anything I wouldn't have told you if you'd come right down that hill sooner and asked. *Kindly.*"

"But—"

"There's no *buts* about it, I don't have the money for your lawyer or time for your trespassing. Get off of my land, or else." He waved the blood-soaked knife in the air, eyes turning to pinpoints as he zeroed in on my eyes. "Go back to where you belong."

"I'm . . ." I backed away, slipping once and falling into the mud. He shook his head, turning back to the kid and working the knife's edge down the thigh to separate the flesh. I swallowed, covering my mouth with my hand to contain my vomit before slipping again.

I glanced down, realizing that it wasn't mud I was slipping in, but the kid's blood.

Horror froze my muscles as I gasped for air. I clamped my teeth down, forcing myself up and turning, eyes crushed closed as I called back to him, "I'm sorry."

He didn't reply.

I didn't blame him.

I wanted to die.

I climbed up the knoll, more careful this time because the shameful tears soaking my vision made everything so blurry.

My dreams to make our life here had been crushed, the situation more hopeless than it had ever been. I stripped before I entered the house again, disbelief that I'd only been gone for less than twenty-five minutes and it felt like twenty-five years. Tommy still slept peacefully, and I was rinsing myself in the outdoor shower when I heard the house alarm bleep once.

My nerves went on high alert, my exchange with Carl earlier coming back to me. I toweled off quickly, wrapping my body tightly, and crept into the house just as I heard Morrissey's comforting whistle coming down the hallway.

I smiled, thankful to have him home after the day I'd had. "Hey there."

He paused, turning his chin at me, a charming smile curling his lips. "Hey, beautiful." He crossed the distance between us, wrapping his arms around me and dotting a kiss on my forehead. "Were you swimming?"

"No," I rushed to answer. "An outdoor shower felt adventurous, I guess."

"Change of scenery." His arms were still around me as he spoke. I loved them about him. I'd missed so many things while I'd been in mourning, but in the last few months, despite everything else going on, he and I had felt closer than ever.

"It's been a rough day."

"A rough year," he mumbled. "But at least we have each other."

He held me close, and I relished the simple moments where he didn't know what I knew.

"I should get dressed." I moved to pull away. "I have to drop some charity stuff off at the newspaper tonight and—"

"Mm, no, stay right here with me." He kissed me softly. "Just. Like. This."

I succumbed, letting him kiss me against the wall, his hands roaming my damp neck as his thumbs grazed my cheekbones.

He was the best kisser.

He was the best everything.

He always had been.

"I can't, I have so much to do."

"But we don't make love anymore." He nipped at my ear.

I froze at his words. "I-I know, it's just, we're so busy and I'm trying to make our dream work and I'm exhausted always and—"

"I know, I know, Lenn. Hear ya loud and clear." He backed away and I missed his arms instantly. I hated myself for making him the enemy in this, I just didn't know another way, other than to make him hate me first.

"Teamwork is key, and I can't be a team when you're gone all the time."

"Team? Lenn, please, I'm trying to keep our other business afloat. Y'know, the one that I sold half the assets of to afford this monster house, and still I'm losing just about everything?"

"I have to get ready." I walked down the hallway, ducking into the walk-in to pull on jeans, a vest, and a sweater.

He didn't follow me.

Part of me wished he had, but most of me knew it was easier this way.

For now.

I walked out of our bedroom a minute later, tracking to the kitchen to find him pouring a double shot of vodka. "I told Carl I'd meet him at nine. I'm gonna spend a few hours polishing the copy and then meet him over there. I have the monitor for Tommy if you need to leave or—"

"I've got him, Lenn. You do you."

CHAPTER THIRTY-FIVE

Morrissey
Seventh night: 11.55 p.m.

Violent cries woke me from a dead sleep.

I shot up, on high alert as I zeroed in on the noise. It echoed from the darkness outside the window. I must have slept all day after cutting my hand. I held still, readjusting to my surroundings as I realized I'd fallen asleep on the couch after Fawn had left. I'd been so tired after sifting through dozens of articles and old police reports on other missing persons cases within a three-hundred-mile radius, I'd crashed out where I sat.

Another shrieking cry split the silence and this time I launched myself to my feet and went for the front door. Throwing it open, a chill ran through me when I realized it was the middle of the night, and here I was, a madman stumbling out into the mist after phantom cries.

Another loud shriek sent me barreling out into the night anyway.

I scanned the darkness, eyes adjusting too slowly.

I felt vulnerable, like the smoke off the water and the dark were swallowing me.

Another sharp cry tore my vision across the yard to land at the front gate, its pillars barely visible in the dark. A thrashing shook the iron and then came another piercing bellow. It sounded unnatural, like something was hurt or dying.

I ducked back into the house and grabbed the grape masher, the first thing my fist clamped around before I raced back into the night.

I was at the gate in under a minute.

A goat, wide-eyed and terrified, blatted at me.

"Scared me to death." I set the masher on the top of the pillar, kneeling to help the small goat untangle his front legs from the bars he'd been fighting to escape through. "You've gotten yourself really stuck, huh?"

I worked to ease him out while he thrashed against my nearness. When I finally had him free, I didn't dare let him go. He was young and active and looked like he'd rather be dead than be with me. I moved my feet quickly, following the top of the knoll that bordered our property before ducking under the fence that usually kept the goats in and hurried down the hill to the farm.

The barnyard was silent, before another goat in the shed sent a call out. The shrill tone, so similar to a crying human baby, set my nerves on edge as I came around the corner of the barn. A slice of yellow light cut through the darkness. I grasped the iron handle with one hand and swung it wide.

What I found sent shockwaves through me.

Goats, goats everywhere, but among them discarded dirty diapers and disposable formula cartons, the stench of human feces rippling the air as it mixed with the odor of goats. "What the hell — is this from Tommy?"

The last thought that crossed my mind before a sharp pain split through my skull and sent my world careening into darkness: the goats.

Kel missed the goats.

CHAPTER THIRTY-SIX

Morrissey
Seventh night: 2.30 a.m.

"You always were useless."

The words played bumper cars in my head. I pressed a hand to my skull, wetness gathering before falling into my eyes and drenching my vision in sticky red.

A numb tingling spread from the crown out, my eyes blinking away the pain as stars sparked and dimmed in front of them. "You took her."

A dry cackle filled the shed.

My head pounded.

"Why?"

"Because I deserve her," the voice seethed. Something pierced my calf and I realized then I was tied to a pole, knees bent and goats jostling around me in their tiny space. "I healed her after you broke her."

"What?" I struggled to wrap my brain around the words.

"You heard me. You never deserved her, not after all the tears she dried in my bed."

"Carl, please, what do you want?"

A malicious laugh overcame his tall form before he landed a kick squarely in my ribcage. "I only want what's mine."

My head bobbed, heavy from holding the weight of it up under the violent throbbing that pressed against my skull. "Carl—"

I couldn't finish my sentence, forced to empty my stomach as the dizziness and pain mingled to create a toxic reaction.

"This whole time?"

"You're damn right. Turns out I'm your worst nightmare, hey, Monroe?"

"How?"

"Only with the support of your wife, that's how."

"You've lost your mind."

"Then why would she leave evidence for me to find, why would she come to me at work late at night, Morrissey? I knew all of her secrets, even the ones she kept from you."

I growled with the truth of his statement.

"Lenn was crying for help from her oldest friend, you can see it on the tapes Kel pulled from the newspaper office — he showed me them. She's crying, you'd devastated her life. Lenn and I were in diapers together, I can read her better than anyone. It only took a few pages of her journal for me to read between the lines."

"There are no lines."

"There are, Morrissey — if there weren't, then why is it that I'm mentioned in her journal quadruple the times you are?"

"Because they're forged. They were meant to steer you off course, Carl, meant to steer both of us off course. And you fell for it. You fell for a scam artist, printed forged words, and helped drive the murderer's narrative. How does it feel?"

"Lenn isn't a scam artist."

"I didn't say it was Lenn." I spit blood into the straw.

"What about Tommy? Tommy is mine, the evidence is in the journals. I know more than you think, and maybe you were the one that was conned by trailer trash. Her heart was already mine, Morrissey. I had her virginity, what else do I need to take to prove it to you?"

"You're not okay, Carl."

"Do you want details of the night she came to me, broken and cast off from the Monroe estate like last night's garbage? How I held her shaking body, naked and warm in my bed? I wouldn't let her become another victim to the Monroe family. When I brought her to my bed, she crawled on top of me and begged me to take away her pain. I've always cleaned up her messes, Morrissey. *All* of her messes."

He didn't give me a chance to reply, only leveled his fist against my cheek and smashed my skull into the wooden pole at my back.

Stars spun like pinwheels in my vision.

"Mamamamamama."

I shook my head, auditory hallucinations overcoming me. Tommy's voice babbled and the goats shuffled and kicked, curious mouths on the pant legs of my jeans, before I felt a palm spread across my forehead and slam my head into the back of the pole again. "What?"

I was groggy, so groggy I couldn't keep it together. I could hardly open my eyes, the pain flashing behind them too erratic to see.

"You're pathetic, that's why you don't deserve them." Carl spit, wetness landing on my cheeks.

Baby babbling filled my ears.

"Tommy?" I grunted, my mind fully losing itself to him. I wondered if I was dreaming all of this, my worst nightmare unfolding in the backyard of my dreams.

Tommy's sweet voice chimed through the air.

"Tommy?" I sagged my head, unable to see anything beyond the bloody blackness. He was real. He was here.

My son, in the arms of the man that had killed my wife.

CHAPTER THIRTY-SEVEN

Morrissey
Seventh night: 2.42 a.m.

"What did you do?"

Tommy's babbling moved farther away and above my head as I realized Carl had picked up my son. I blinked away the blood, forcing my eyelids open. Focusing was impossible; I could only make out a tall blur hovering over me, a tiny bright yellow form in his arms.

Tommy must have his rain jacket on, the school-bus yellow coat a perfect match to the hat — the same I'd found floating the night of his disappearance.

"Tommy!" I called, but my voice came out garbled, like whatever he'd hit me with had caused whiplash hard enough to crush my windpipe.

"Dada," Tommy sang happily. He seemed so comfortable in Carl's arms, the realization that he must have been there before and often was like a bucket of ice to my senses.

"Tommy, do you see your mama, buddy? Lenn? Lenn!"

"Shut up." Carl circled my throat with his hand. "I don't ever want to hear her name on your lips again. This is my family."

Tommy chattered. Carl set him down in the straw and I sensed the group of goats gathering around him, investigating.

"Carl, where is she? Just tell me she's safe, I don't care if you want to be together. I'll give her the divorce, whatever you both want."

Carl scoffed, kicking straw in my face. I spit out the dirty strands, vowing silently to bury his head in the ground if I ever caught him.

He picked Tommy up again, this time tossing him in the air and catching him to cause my boy to erupt into giggles.

Giggles that shattered my heart.

"Those journal pages you printed, they were fake — it all makes sense now. It didn't at first, but now I see you got played—"

"I didn't get played." I could hear the indignation in Carl's voice. I just had to hope I didn't piss him off enough to hurt Tommy. If I could just keep him distracted and talking, maybe I could work my wrists out of the zip ties.

"Oh, sure you did. I don't know where those fake journal pages came from, but I know they're not Lenn's—"

"How do you know? You don't know her at all."

"She's my wife, I know her better than anyone."

"She has secrets."

"Everyone has secrets, I'm fine with secrets. We're secure enough in our marriage — I trust the things she doesn't tell me are for good reason."

"No." Carl's voice was shaking now. "You ran your family into the ground before my son was even born."

The fact was, Carl maybe did know a few more things about my wife from the past, but he didn't know her heart. "How can you be Tommy's father when you weren't in the birthing room with Lenn, when you didn't hear him take his first breaths or watch him take his first steps? I'll have all his firsts because I'm there, Carl. That's what counts."

"You say that now, but I'm not the one zip-tied to a pole with a bleeding head wound." He held Tommy tightly as I worked the zip ties against a rusty nail sticking out of the pole at my back. "Maybe that's why you have such trouble remembering the worst night of my life?"

"Your worst . . . what are you talking about?" I edged the zip tie over one of the bones in my wrist, trying not to wince as pain shot through my nerves.

"The night you lied to the law and justice wasn't served."

"Why are you talking in riddles?"

"The night you almost killed my sister." He was fuming now, leaning closer to me. "The night you stole everything from me."

"I don't know what you're talking about."

"Of course you don't, it was probably just another day in your spoiled life — but my life was never the same. You stole the most precious thing from me, and then you did it again a few years later, and so—" his grin twisted — "now karma has come a-callin'."

"What did I steal, Carl? I'll make it right, whatever it is."

"It's too late."

My vision came into clearer focus. I could see Tommy, resting his head on Carl's shoulder as he sucked on his little fist.

"The night Kel nearly drove my sister off the bluff, she broke her collarbone and suffered a spinal injury that changed her forever. She might as well be dead."

"What?"

"It's like you weren't even there," Carl snarled. "Take a life and then forget about it, does that skill come along with the inheritance when you're a Monroe?"

"I remember the night, Carl, but I can't figure out what it has to do with you."

"Because after Deputy Kendry dropped off the tourist at the campground that night, he picked up my sister. It was starting to rain and she refused to get on my bike, but then Kel came along. He could do anything and she'd follow him — she liked him so much it made me sick that he didn't even know her name."

"Carl, he knew her name, please—"

"He didn't! He told them it was a drunk tourist girl in the front seat and it wasn't — it was my sister. He almost killed her and he was too drunk to even realize it."

"Carl, please, this doesn't have anything to do with Lenn—"

"It has everything to do with her. Lies always unravel, Monroe. Didn't your dad ever teach you that? Hard lesson to learn, isn't it?"

"You're right, you're right, okay? I shouldn't have lied. I didn't think Kel had had that much to drink, but he was so drunk and confused the next morning, I think he'd blacked out that night — he didn't even know he'd been in an accident until I called to ask how he was doing the next afternoon."

"Bullshit. He walked away while she left on a stretcher and he didn't care."

"He didn't know."

"He didn't bother to ask, because let's face it, how does it look if the sheriff and lead deputy on the police force are both crooked?"

His voice cracked as he backed away to the door. I used the momentary aversion of his eyes to work the zip ties more quickly against the nail, praying I could find a sharp edge to cut the hard plastic.

"She spent months in therapy, but she never walked again. She was sent to a care home and never advanced beyond the ninth-grade education she had when you almost took her life."

"I-I didn't."

"You lied to Kel's dad — we were all drinking that night at the water, and you told him Kel wasn't, that he was the designated driver, but Kel had had as many shots as any of us."

His words triggered a memory, a memory of that night, the stars, Lenn, the water — but I couldn't remember the tourist girl. Or Carl, or anyone else that night for that matter.

I felt a bone break in my hand before my wrist slipped fully out of the zip tie. I nearly slumped forward with relief but caught myself before Carl noticed.

"You lied to the police, and my family could never press charges or receive the insurance coverage for the accident because, according to public record, there was no accident. It was only a slide-off with no evidence to implicate Kel. You lied to the sheriff that night, and because he was the sheriff, he had the authority to write it off . . . and so he did."

His words cut through me, emotion flooding my eyes as the puzzle pieces finally came together. Carl's hatred was justified.

"No one ever knew, never even cared about her, except Lenn. She's the only one that ever asked how Jenny was, she even came to visit when Jenny was home for Christmas dinner one year."

The constant generosity of my wife was just one of the things I'd fallen so hard for about her, and now . . . well, I knew I wasn't good enough for her, and I never had been. Some in town may have expressed curiosity when Lenn and I got married; our lives across the tracks were more different than alike, but not in the ways it mattered.

I'd always felt that she really saw me, but apparently Carl felt she saw him too.

"So, what happens when I'm gone? You'll marry my wife? Live happily ever after?" I asked.

"We'll make our own family."

"And what happens to Tommy? Will you be tested?"

"Tested?"

"To confirm paternity — you're so sure, but I imagine risking so much, you'd want assurances."

"I don't have to wonder, I know when Lenn and I were together. The timelines make sense, Tommy is my boy."

"But what if he isn't, Carl? What if he's a Monroe?"

I winced when Carl thrust the sleepy Tommy in the air, no longer giggles but scared cries filling the shed. Carl kept throwing him higher and higher, a smile finally tilting his lips when he snarled, "If I found out Tommy was a Monroe, then maybe a horrible accident would come to him. His blood is tainted with liars and thieves. Lenn and I would make a family that's pure and true and born of love, not the sickness you brought to her life." Carl snuggled Tommy close and murmured in his ear until his tears turned to soft sniffles.

The muscles in my body twitched to launch into action but I had to wait until Carl turned, I had to give myself at least a shot at knocking him out, otherwise . . . otherwise . . . I began to wonder how I could do both, knock him out and catch Tommy before he fell.

"I need you to sign Titan over to me, Morrissey." Carl threw a rolled-up wad of papers at me. I clenched my teeth when I saw the logo of our mortgage company and the bank the company was financed through on the various letterheads.

"Did Lenn give you these?" I would have crumbled and signed it all over to him right then if he'd give me my boy back. He and Lenn could have it all, as long as I had Tommy safe in my arms.

"Where else would I get them?" He spit and whipped a pen at me.

I bit my tongue, realizing if I told him I couldn't sign tied to a post, he'd come to release me and realize I wasn't — but then maybe he'd set Tommy down and I could take my chance.

I began to pray for whatever outcome saved my son.

Just as I was about to tell him to untie me, a shadowy figure appeared behind Carl. A swinging shovel and a solid *thunk* of a skull cracking against wood echoed throughout the shed.

Carl slumped, Tommy falling gently down to the floor along with him.

The shadow picked up my son, tucking his bright yellow form against his hip. "There you are, little guy."

CHAPTER THIRTY-EIGHT

Morrissey
Seventh night: 3.17 a.m.

I shot off the floor, goats scattering and mewling as I swiped my son from the arms of the stranger.

"Was wondering what the ruckus was out there, the goats have been on edge all night." He lowered his hood, the weathered face of the goat farmer haunting the shadows of the shed. The goats gathered around his legs, crying even more loudly. He waved them off with his shovel, before grabbing one of Carl's ankles and dragging him through the straw and mud and out into the barnyard.

"Did you know?"

"No more than you did." He grunted, shuffling across the straw floor. "Can't say it should be much of a surprise after what you kids pulled on the bluff."

"Come again?"

"You know what I mean. Spoiled brats turned criminals the night you almost killed the girl on the bluff. You got off once after I called the police. It's always been about pathetic last names in this town, so am I surprised you're here? Not really, not when vicious rumors and reckless lies consume your mind more than an honest day of work ever did. You all needed a damn good lesson if you ask me."

I watched as he bent over Carl. The realization that this man had somehow witnessed that foggy night on the bluff two years ago was shocking, but less so when I thought of how many times I'd caught shadows his size and stature hobbling around by moonlight.

The discomforting realization set in that some people in this town knew my life better than I did.

"What if he comes to? Should we zip-tie his wrists?"

"He won't." He stood. "He doesn't have a pulse."

Tommy snored softly on my shoulder, none the wiser to the chaos around him.

"I guess I should call the police—"

Before I could finish my sentence, a shadow split the moonlight in the doorway, a solid *thunk* landing at the back of the farmer's head before he fell awkwardly to the ground.

"Hey!" I was almost out of the shed before I realized I held Tommy.

"Hey there, son," a woman's voice hummed. "Or should I say . . . son-in-law." She stepped into the moonlight, an unmistakably familiar angle to her jaw, a wild twinkle in her eye. "We haven't had the privilege of meeting, I'm Lennox's mother."

Tommy mumbled awake on my shoulder, eyes flickering open to land on the woman that stood just feet across from me.

"Hey there, Tommy, wanna play with Grandma?" Lenn's mom, Sheryl, cooed to my boy and a soft smile crossed his lips. He held one tiny fist out to the woman, fat fingers reaching to her before he settled back into my neck.

"Where's Lenn?"

"You don't think Carl killed her?" She smiled sweetly and it sent a chill down my spine. She swayed on her feet, tapping something in the palm of her hand. The grape masher. The one I'd left at the gate, the one that was covered in someone's blood.

"Should I think that?"

"Well, sweet son-in-law, it's been so murdery around the Point lately, and all signs seem to point to you. Lennox's blood on your hands sounds like an open and shut case. I made sure to wear gloves when I handled the grape masher I found in your barn." She wiggled the gloved fingers of one hand at me like a wicked witch with a matching sinister smile. "I thought leaving the Hollows wine bottle covered in blood was a nice touch. I thought for sure they'd arrest you then, but Officer Kendry is just so incompetent it's criminal. He's not protecting the people of this town, letting your family get away with rape and murder. You think the working-class folks are too simple to understand how your legacy was built on their labor before you destroyed them, but they see. They see, and they're just too smart to say anything."

I held Tommy a little closer. "It was just business."

"Business. It was never about business. You're a fool, just like your father. Lennox was so eager to marry into your family, but I knew it was the start of the worst days of her life. I tried to tell her, tried to make her see that morning she came home after—" Something caught her attention behind her then and I used the diversion to register the farmer's shovel still resting against the pole I'd been tied to minutes ago.

I gulped, realizing my only hope was leaping across a dozen goats to grab that without her seeing, while keeping Tommy safely in one arm.

Circumstances seemed hopeless.

And then the worst happened.

The soft thud of a body on clay, a dragging noise, gentle garbled noises and then I saw it.

The one thing that I'd been fearing all along.

Lenn.

Dead.

CHAPTER THIRTY-NINE

Morrissey
Seventh night: 3.35 a.m.

"No." Sheryl laughed, the shrill noise startling Tommy awake. He began crying instantly, digging deeper into my chest as he wailed.

"Tommmmy!" Lenn's formerly still body came to life, trying to come to her knees even though her hands were tied.

"Lenn!" I dove to her, first tearing the remaining slash of duct tape from her mouth. "Are you okay?!"

I tried to feel frantically on the ground for a sharp rock to cut the zip tie at her wrists. "I bet the goat farmer has a pocket knife in his pants."

Lenn nodded, eyes teary and frantic.

I snuggled Tommy against Lenn's body, all the while keeping my eyes on Sheryl, hovering above the bodies of two dead men.

"Why all the theatrics? Why now?" I stood, backing against the wall of the shed.

If she turned away from me for even a second, I could dodge back into the shed and grab the shovel.

And then what? Murder Lenn's mom?

I needed a miracle.

"Men," she spit.

"Carl was there for me in the most traumatic moment of my life, and you just . . . used him, used his feelings to get to me?" Lenn choked.

"Carl was too stupid to love you, he was a liability with all of those emotions. How could he ever protect you and Tommy? If anything, I've given you another gift, one less problem off your hands. And Spalding, I thought I could rely on him to keep a secret and hack your security system. He sent me the footage of that night after adding what I told him to add, and I had full access to all the cameras in your house right from my phone — it's brilliant what these little apps can do nowadays. Morrissey was like my little monkey, with just a finger swipe I had him so on edge. So then I had to have a little fun and added that pathetic song he hates." She turned to me. "Lenn told me everything about that night. I figured waking up to the song your dad had hung himself to would send you over the edge . . . but you just weren't making enough mistakes. I thought you'd take more pills, I knew if I could get you to take more you'd walk right into your own trap, but then Kel kept sticking up for you—"

"He's had his hands full, thanks to you," I said.

A proud smile cut her thin lips. "I'm quite the choreographer, aren't I?"

"Well, I wouldn't go that far."

"What do you mean?"

"If your goal was to have me in jail for Lenn's murder . . ." I shrugged.

Her face stretched taut, teeth bared in a growl. "That's why I had to kill Spalding. He didn't listen, didn't follow my plan. He was supposed to keep Tommy across the bay at the old fish camp in the woods, but Tommy cried too much and Spalding ran out of money for diapers and bottles, and no matter what I brought him, nothing helped. I tried to visit every night, and then I realized Lenn was digging a hole through the basement wall of the lighthouse so I couldn't leave her ever—"

"The lighthouse? Lenn, were you at the lighthouse this entire time?"

"I thought Tommy was dead this entire time." I could hear the neglect in her voice, like she hadn't been given water in days.

One of the baby goats came over then, snuggling closer to a sleeping Tommy, before folding its legs under itself and settling its head on Tommy's belly. So at home, like he was used to my boy being right here.

I remembered the bottles and spare diapers scattered in the shed. "Did you keep Tommy here?"

She shrugged. "I needed to be near enough to see what you were going to do. It was easy, Hank has been lonely out here on the Point all of these years, he enjoyed some company and my fresh-baked banana bread. We caught up, it'd been years since we'd had a conversation. The more I stopped by the more he opened up about the two of you."

"Did Kel know?"

"Of course not. I just stopped in to bring him something nice to snack on now and again. It's funny, the things a man sees when nobody sees him. He knows so much about you. It's sad how little you really knew about the only other human living way out here with you, don't you think?"

I grit my teeth, wondering if this could have all been avoided by reaching out to our only neighbor more than we had, more than just for what we wanted from him.

"I wish . . . there are a lot of things I would do differently if I could."

"Like keeping your father's disgusting hands off of my daughter?"

Confusion radiated through my system. "W-what?"

Her shrill cackle woke both Tommy and the sleeping goat, and both cried. Tears streaked Lenn's face as I noticed her shifting back and forth against something. A small pile of rusted junk in the grass behind her caught my attention.

"You still don't know, after the journals and everything. You didn't piece the night together?"

"No!" Lenn bleated, body slumping as she cried over Tommy. "Please don't do this. Not after everything."

"Yes, after everything. Truth is the only way forward." Sheryl's deceptively moral words froze me to the spot. "Your father didn't just rape this town of its pensions and livelihood, he raped my daughter the night before he hung himself. You were so busy thinking about yourself that you never thought to ask why she ran away that night, why she came home with tears in her eyes and the smell of a grown man on her skin. I just assumed it was you, Morrissey, that'd hurt my baby. I wasn't right, but I wasn't quite wrong either. The Monroe bloodline is tainted, my grandson born of that disgusting night when your family stole the last remaining light that shone down on mine."

"No!" I fell to my knees, crippled by her insinuations. "No, my father—"

"Your father was a rapist. He died a criminal and he knew it — that's why he hung himself." She lunged, grape masher pressed against my neck and her hot words at my ear. "He didn't care an ounce that he hobbled this town with his dirty money. I don't even think he cared that he took the only thing my daughter had to give to ensure her future — I think he cared that he would get caught for it." I gasped for breath as she pressed down on my windpipe. "And I think you didn't care to ask why because you didn't want to know. It's hard to inherit millions from a criminal that bankrupted a town."

"Lenn," I moaned.

"It's too late for talk. I took matters into my own hands to show Lenn just the kind of man she married. I needed Carl's access — he's more powerful than he knows at the newspaper, and he just handed it all over to me." She shrugged. "And then I was able to file a complaint against you as a sex offender, anonymously of course. It was so easy, and then there's that little sticky note I made sure found its way to your front porch when it needed to."

I wrenched her off of me. My hands slipped through the grass, finally locking around an old iron bar that had been hidden beneath straw and mud. "You're, you're—"

"Not a criminal." She smiled almost sweetly, and for the first time it hit me that I was dealing with a severely mentally unstable person. Someone who didn't care that they might be — that felt morally empowered, morally untouchable. "I've done nothing wrong that you can prove."

Cold wind whipped the door on the shed, clattering against the booted foot of the goat farmer as blood darkened and pooled the dirt under his body.

She'd murdered a man, and she didn't seem to care.

"I knew you didn't feel safe enough to tell me then. I get it, Lennox, I hadn't been there. I had a talk with your dad and then I left, I knew I couldn't help you like you needed. Not then, but now. Now I'm stronger in my vows to raise you."

"Vows? You never even spoke to me all those times you left, Dad and I barely made it though most weeks and you, you just . . . went off and partied."

"I wasn't partying, Lennox, far from it." Her eyes sparkled with some moral knowing. "I was finding myself. And so I knew I had to come back and be the mom I was never strong enough to be before. That man stole everything from this town. Evil runs in bloodlines, Lennox — your daddy didn't bring you up with any God-fearin' ways, but that's why I'm here now."

"You locked me in a lighthouse basement and kidnapped my son!"

"I had to do what was necessary to show you that Morrissey wasn't the man for you. He's not good enough for my baby — I had to expose the evil at his core."

"Evil?" Lenn quivered, her dirty fingers trembling and chapped with the cold. "You murdered an innocent teenager just because he couldn't carry out your evil plan to murder my baby?"

"Your baby was born of evil. I did what I did for the greater good."

"He isn't evil," she gasped, eyes shut tight as she seemed to flashback to an earlier, more painful time. She said the next words so softly I almost thought I imagined them. "My baby was born of love."

"I know Carl says you had an affair, but I knew you'd just lied to him to keep him off—"

"No!" Lenn yelled. "I did try to keep him off, I tried. I didn't know what to say anymore because he believed none of it, and all I ever gave him was the truth." Sheryl stiffened. "Is Tommy Carl's baby?"

Lenn's face scrunched up, head bent to the ground before she breathed, "He is not."

"I knew it, I knew he was Frank Monroe's."

"The timing lines up, but you're wrong . . ."

"I'm not wrong. It's as I thought all along, evil runs in the blood, and that man let you fall victim to his father, and then he stole your heart and walked all over it after you vowed your life to him. No woman should vow her life to anyone but God. Man is so very fallible, Lennox, haven't I taught you anything?"

Lenn was shaking, something like shock settling into her limbs. A chilled mist was creeping inland, weakening my muscles, turning my blood to sludge in my veins and weighting my limbs. I prayed Kel would arrive soon. I prayed Sheryl would make a mistake and I could take her out with the iron bar and get my family back to safety.

"I knew the evil had manifested itself again when I saw you burying something on the knoll one night. I thought for sure you'd done something bad, Lenn. Don't get me wrong, I thought I might find Tommy buried in those sheets." She crowed with wicked laughter. "I had no idea what to expect, but, when I found the bloody sheets and the journals, I just knew Morrissey had let you down again. I knew he'd raped and brutalized you and you were suffering in silence. I knew then they must have blackmailed you into marrying into the very family that victimized you to save face and keep you quiet. And you, so proud and noble, unwilling to walk away. This is me giving you a path to walk away on, sweet girl."

"Is that what you did when I was little?" Lenn grunted.

"What do you mean?"

"Kel told me what he found, he told me you had an affair with his dad and so he covered up the fact that you *kidnapped* me when I was just a baby."

"That's not true, I was just proving a lesson to your dad that he wasn't ready to be a parent. He needed me. *You* needed me."

"You kept me locked up on a stranger's boat without food for three days. I spent days in the hospital with Dad and the police at my side . . . and while everyone thought there was a horrible kidnapper on the loose, you were flirting with the town sheriff so he wouldn't press charges." Sheryl rolled her eyes. "A mother does what she has to do."

I was fuming now, so many secrets that Lenn knew and hadn't revealed, so many lies.

"So, what about the affair with Carl?" I ventured.

Lenn shook her head. "There was no affair, there never was."

That realization loosened my muscles, fear evaporating into numb resignation. I knew nothing about the woman I loved. Had I just not asked the right questions?

"I went to Carl a few days after your father—" she swallowed — "after your father raped me in the pool house. I was too ashamed to tell you, I thought it was my fault, a misunderstanding. But I couldn't go home because I knew Dad would kill whoever had left bruises on my skin . . ."

"So . . . you and Carl?"

I saw her wince in the darkness. "I didn't know what to do . . ."

"Lenn's string of lies, more perfect than a set of pearls," Sheryl chuckled. "It only took me one quick conversation with Carl at the newspaper office to realize he thought you had raped Lennox that night. I forced Lennox to tell me everything that night in the lighthouse — it was the best talk we've had in a while, wasn't it, baby?" She smiled, as if proud of the relationship she was creating with her daughter. "We were so lucky that Hank is the keeper of the light and had the keys. It was a gift, all that time he gave us together. I'm so sad to see it end now." Her words struck an ominously happy tone.

"You stole the keys to the lighthouse from him?" I was stupefied by the way she'd masterminded this.

"Of course not, I only made a few copies. I had the master back in his desk before he realized it was gone. You know, when I thought my baby was being abused again—"

"This is why I can't tell you anything," Lenn grit, and I couldn't help the twitch of my lips with the dash of sarcasm in my wife's words. Even bound and tied, she was there, fighting. "You need help, Mother."

"No, no, don't you see: I only saw an opportunity when I ran into Hank at the grocery store. We got to talking and I realized he was right up here on the Point with you — I realized I finally had a chance to truly be in my daughter's life again. You know, Gigi is so close and spends so much time with Tommy, teaching him swimming and babysitting all the time, I wanted to help you in my own way."

"By ruining the only life I'd built for myself?" Lenn's tone was soft but accusing.

"No, baby, I'm rescuing you from yourself."

CHAPTER FORTY

Morrissey
Seventh night: 4.15 a.m.

"The night Morrissey found the journals was a test — the perfect test." Sheryl stood above her daughter, the grape masher smacking her palm loudly. "I suspected he was too proud to call the police, too cowardly to show evidence that proved his wife had had an affair — and that's exactly what he did. When I noticed on the security footage that he'd found the journals and hadn't called Kel to report it, I knew it was time." Her eyes sparkled with malevolence. "I made sure the journal pages that shared the details of the affair with Carl landed in the right hands at the right time."

I staggered toward the woman that had nearly stolen my family from me. "You stole the pages? You had them printed and my family's name slandered all over town?"

"It's hard to slander when it's the truth." Her eyes turned wild as she lunged, swinging the masher at my head. I ducked, trying to reach for her ankle but missing, before she landed the tip of the metal in the center of my calf.

I lashed out in pain, screaming so loudly a group of goats started bleating into the darkness. No matter how much we shouted, we were out here all alone with this madwoman.

"You should know me better than that, son," she seethed. "I found just the right messenger for the job."

My brain ached with her riddles. I had no idea what she meant by "the right messenger," only that she'd conjured such a horrific ruse, I should be ready for anything.

"This would have been easier if you'd taken the opportunity to kill yourself when I gave it to you like your good-for-nothing father did. I'd hoped that song would push you over the edge, but you're tougher than I gave you credit for. I knew you were too proud to call the police as long as it implicated you. You weren't interested in the truth any more than anyone else. I only had to plant the idea in Carl's head that Lenn was afraid for her life — it wasn't hard after finding the bloody sheets — and he was ready to be her knight in shining armor again. I told him Lenn confronted you about the affair with the high school girl and you hit her, such a mean streak in that Monroe family. Carl was truly the brave one, Lenn, he gave up so much for you, more than you know. What's that saying — the road to hell is laid with good intentions? Rest in peace, Carl."

She made a small sign of the cross against her chest and I cringed.

"So, the test — it was brilliant, I was so proud of it. Because Morrissey, once I had you second-guessing reality and I knew you wouldn't go running to Kel to bail you out, I had you where I wanted you. So, I hooked the baby goat in the gate. I'd hoped it would trigger your alarm system, but the crying was even better for dramatic effect. Lenn and I could hear it from our view on the bay, couldn't we, sweetheart? Watching you run out there was a hoot."

Delight turned her cheeks rosy. She was demented, and her blood ran through the veins of my son.

"So you see, Morrissey, the night you found the journals and didn't call the police, you failed my little test . . ." She giggled like a schoolgirl that had outwitted a classmate. "Or *passed*, depending on what side of the coin you fall on, I s'pose."

CHAPTER FORTY-ONE

Morrissey
Seventh night: 4.25 a.m.

"Morrissey . . ." Lenn grimaced, holding her stomach as she shivered in the grass. "Baby . . ."

Rage roared to life inside of me, my muscles snapping back into awareness as I launched across the mud to knock Sheryl off-kilter.

She crashed into a bale of straw. "Sign Titan over, Morrissey. Sign the business bank account over to me or so help me, I will make you regret the day you met my family." She swung wildly. "Thieves Cove deserves their pensions, the Monroes are thieves."

Realization suddenly snapped into place. I'd imagined Lenn was looking to refinance the house, but it probably had something to do with this woman here, now that I knew the sinister ways she'd inserted herself quietly into our lives.

"Sign the papers, give my daughter what's owed, what your family took away from us." She was blabbering, nearly incoherent but still stronger and more vicious than she looked. "You'll be sitting in jail soon. Kel will be here any minute to arrest you for Spalding Thurston's murder, and then he'll see what you did to Carl, how you maimed your poor neighbor to keep your secrets." Sheryl swung the masher square at my jaw. I coughed a spray of blood into the air and nearly vomited with the pain.

"I just wanted to have it all. Being a wife and mom took so much, I just wanted to be the best grandma."

I slumped, stars sparkling through my vision as my body swayed with a dim tingling sensation, warm wetness traveling down my cheek and neck in rivers.

"Don't ever doubt a mother's love, Monroe." Sheryl held the grape masher back and Lenn shrieked in the distance before another sound echoed off the barnyard walls.

Bang.

CHAPTER FORTY-TWO

Morrissey
Eighth day: 7.30 a.m.

"Why don't you start from the top?" Kel sat back in the folding chair in the back room of the precinct.

"The top?"

"Day one."

"Well, day one really starts with night one." Lenn wrung her hands together under the table. I laced our fingers, sending her support however I could.

"I dropped off the charity registration papers and graphic design mockup advertising Pumpkin Fest for Lakeshore Academy Daycare. We have Tommy signed up to start there next fall, but we wanted to make the effort ahead of time in the hope that he would be accepted into the exclusive Montessori-based early development program, so I offered up my meager business skills for free. I thought I'd be in and out that night at the newspaper, but Carl wasn't having it. He started telling these lies — well, I thought they were lies. He's become so unpredictable lately I didn't dream he was telling the truth."

"The truth about what?" Kel urged gently.

"Th-that my mom had come to see him, saying she was worried about my safety — that Morrissey was hurting me and I needed an escape plan to leave him. I was so angry that he would say that — he of all people knew how sensitive I was about the stuff with my mom, I just couldn't believe he would bring her up now. I thought he only wanted to get a rise out of me, so we got in this huge fight. I accused him of being a liar and then he swore that he loved me and he tried to kiss me and I pushed him off and—"

"He tried to kiss you?" Kel frowned. "You're sure?"

Lenn nodded fiercely.

"That's odd, we pulled the tapes from that night and saw the argument, but I don't recall a kiss."

My heart thundered as I wondered what Kel was thinking.

"He did try to kiss me, Kel. Maybe you had a bad angle."

"Or maybe the tape was edited," I offered.

"Maybe." Kel frowned then gestured for Lenn to continue.

"I was so upset when I drove home that night, I took the turns extra slow. I almost thought about pulling over. I was so angry at Carl for putting me in this position again. We shared one night, one night I regret — one night where I tried to use him to erase a bad memory and . . . and he never forgave me."

I thought about excusing myself at that point, unwilling to hear any more retellings of her and Carl's night together. Between the journals and Carl himself, I'd had enough details to last a lifetime. I didn't understand why she did it, but I knew Lenn, and I knew her heart was always in the right place, even if it was misguided.

"I came home like normal, let myself in, but I had no idea that Carl had followed me in on his bike. The entire way he'd cycled behind my car. It sounds like a sweet gesture by a lovesick boyfriend, but I realize now he was so deranged. In a blink, he went from being my safe place to being . . . my captor."

"He kidnapped you then?"

Fresh tears fell. "He didn't have to, he took Tommy." Her shoulders began to shake as I tried to hold her steady.

"I don't think she's eaten much, Kel, can we finish this later?"

"No, no, I can't prolong this anymore," Lenn cried. "Carl hid in the house until I was in the bathroom about to change into my pajamas. I wouldn't have even noticed immediately, except the video monitor flickered to life when I heard rustling noises in Tommy's room. A shadow caught my eye and by the time I was in the hallway, they were already out of the doors and running down the path to the bay. I just launched into action. I didn't even think to scream — I didn't know who it was, I wasn't sure if they had Tommy at that point. I just followed them right down to the shoreline. I was barefoot and fell twice down the hill, and I still couldn't see anything because the fog off the bay was so thick that night. I didn't see anything until I caught sight of Tommy's yellow jacket in the moonlight. Then I knew, someone had kidnapped my son."

"So you never woke Morrissey up? Not through any of this?"

She shook her head.

"And you didn't think to call the police from the boathouse — there is a phone line in the boathouse, isn't there? I'm sure I saw one when we combed it the first day."

"Yes, there is, but I didn't think . . . I just saw his little yellow body go off the dock and I ran after him, prepared to jump in and swim if I had to—"

"Lenn, you can't swim."

"I can, I practiced. I've been swimming for months on my own in the early morning, building my strength. I wanted to surprise you, but then . . . then—"

"So you *do* know how to swim? Because when Morrissey said you didn't know how that first day, it's one of the reasons that made me suspect him more — an accidentally drowned wife, tale as old as time." A look of disdain crossed his features.

"I can swim a little — not far, but enough." Lenn cleared her throat.

Kel wrote something down on his pad, circling it three times. I squinted to make out the scratch but wasn't able to. I wondered if cops in movies did that just to intimidate the suspect; it felt like that, even now, when I wasn't a suspect.

"But before I could jump in the water to swim after Tommy and whoever had him in that boat, I was hit over the head and knocked out. I don't remember anything else. The next thing I came to, staring at a cement wall of photos, my mother holding a bloody hammer over my head and telling me my son and husband were dead."

CHAPTER FORTY-THREE

Morrissey
Eighth day: 7.40 a.m.

"So, you didn't know it was Carl that had taken your son?"

"Not at that point, but Mom told me later — long after she let me believe that Tommy was dead — that Carl had something to do with it because he loved me and wanted revenge on Morrissey." Lenn worked her bandaged hand absentmindedly.

Her mother had smashed her finger with the vintage grape masher, just to leave evidence for Kel's crew to find in the boathouse. Her wound was gnarly. Black and blue and bandaged tightly so the bones would fuse correctly now, she'd fractured at least three bones in her pinky finger alone.

I'd already teased her that she would have a scar worthy of an evil villain by the time it was healed.

A permanent memory of her nightmare.

"I couldn't piece together how my mom had all of these half-brained stories, I still can't, but knowing now she'd spent time with the goat farmer before that night, just watching and planning . . ." A visible shudder coursed through Lenn's shoulders. Kel had already informed us that a search of Carl's trailer revealed empty baby bottles and diapers and a mattress that looked like the one that had flashed on my security footage that day in the kitchen. Tommy had been right under our noses. And the hours that Carl was working at the newspaper, Tommy was either left alone in the spare room, or Sheryl spent the day with him. "She led me to believe you were dead, that the goat farmer had killed you already, and she kept talking about my future and how I didn't need a washed-up family's filthy wealth to have a good life. She kept saying that she, Tommy, and I could move away and start over and give the Monroe blood money back to Thieves Cove. She was so focused on the money, but she's fooling nobody. I've never met a less charitable person — she'll never give a dime away to anyone. Her ability to swoop into town for a few days and burn through my dad's bank account is legend. I guess it's no wonder she found someone else to move onto that suited her needs."

"And she and Hank were friends back in high school."

"What?" Lenn asked.

"Well, that's what Hank told me when I questioned him the night you disappeared. When I asked if he had any connection to your family, he mentioned that he and Lenn's dad went way back to their high school days. Hadn't seen him in years though. I guess I assumed that meant he hadn't seen anyone in years, alone up at the Point and all."

"The entire time she rowed us across the bay last night, with my mouth duct taped, she described how the goat farmer had buried Tommy and you together under our vineyard and that's what they would do to me someday . . . she just wanted to torture us."

Lenn was shaking, and I wrapped her up in my arms.

"She's in jail now, Lennox. She can't hurt you anymore, I promise you that."

"Someone in your department already promised my father that once before," Lenn replied.

Kel's eyes widened. "I told you that in confidence, Lenn, to be helpful. Don't betray me now, this is all on camera."

"I wish that night had been on camera, the night your father found me in a boat with that woman, the night he let a child abuser walk free. Or if your dad would have had a body camera the night Carl's sister was hurt — maybe things would be different, maybe your lies would have caught up to you a little sooner."

Kel's hands shook now. "You don't know what you're saying, Lenn."

"I know exactly what I'm saying."

Kel rubbed at his knee, a pained look on his face as if the mental reminder brought back the physical sensations.

"Sheriff Kendry, why don't we start talking evidence — haven't these people been tortured enough?" Fawn waltzed into the room and threw her briefcase onto the table. "Did forensics get back with the DNA on that grape masher yet?"

"She was wearing gloves, Fawn. So far all we've found are Morrissey's fingerprints, Lenn's *old* blood, and Morrissey's blood from tonight. I don't think there's any big picture here you need to be concerned with. I drove up just in time to shoot the handle of the masher out of Sheryl's hand — I saw what I saw."

"So, there's absolutely no suspicion about the whereabouts of my client in relation to that grape masher the night his wife went missing?"

"No, of course not, but it's suspicious as hell that you didn't come forward when you found it and the journals. I don't know what you were thinking, withholding information on an active investigation."

"I wasn't thinking, and I wasn't sure it would help."

"Well, Sheryl sure seemed to cover her bases as far as forensic evidence goes. All we have is Lenn's word. Unless we find the original security footage that shows Carl taking Tommy or Lenn getting hit over the head at the boathouse, or Sheryl reburying those journals out back of your house that night—"

"There isn't any. She had Spalding Thurston turn the cameras off the night they planned to take Tommy. I don't know if he knew what my mom had planned, but from the few things that slipped out while she was with me in the lighthouse, it seems like she probably told him the same story she told Carl — that I was in danger and needed help."

"So he helped by turning off the security camera?" I uttered.

"He was paid to help, and apparently not very much. Not even enough to take care of Tommy. I guess she forgot he'd need to eat."

I grit my teeth, thinking of the horror my poor son had faced, picturing that grainy image of the baby on the mattress. The urge to whisk my family far away from here was powerful. Overwhelmingly so.

"Do you think your crime scene unit missed the bloody grape masher in the boathouse, Kendry?" Fawn raised an eyebrow.

Kel puffed out his cheeks, standing up from his chair and shaking his head. "Absolutely not, it's the force's position that the grape masher was planted later by Sheryl in an attempt to frame Morrissey."

"Good." Fawn stepped closer, glaring down at him. "If I catch wind of you withholding anything in this case, Sheriff, I'll have you and the entire department's heads."

Kel fumed, nostrils flaring as he crossed his arms, but gave no reply.

"Okay, we're done with this pissing contest." I stood, Lenn in my arms as we crossed the small interrogation room. Fawn yanked her briefcase over her shoulder, following us out before telling us to call her if we needed anything.

I hoped we wouldn't.

"I'm truly sorry if there's anything me or my department did to upset you more, Lenn." Kel opened the door of our Audi SUV, letting Lenn slip up into the passenger seat before closing the door behind her. Her window rolled down, she patted his forearm, squeezing it once and smiling softly.

"Thank you for everything, Kel, I just need some rest. I hope Tommy and I can forget this nightmare ever happened.

Please, let me know when you find out about Carl's funeral arrangements too, I want to take care of them. You pick out the casket, but send the bill to me, okay?"

"You were good to him. I don't know if he deserved it."

"He did, Kel, we all do." She wiped at the corner of her eye. "I'm still struggling with the boy I grew up with going down such a dark path . . . I don't really understand it, I felt so safe with him for so long."

A sad smile split Kel's features. "He wanted the best for you, even in the end. I forgot to tell you, but the reason I found you at the goat shed was because of him."

"What?" Confusion traced Lenn's face. "How?"

"He sent me a text. I didn't get the message until my alarm woke me up for my shift this morning, and I wasn't sure what to make of it at first — just GPS coordinates. Until I plugged them into my map software and realized where he was pointing me to — right at the shed. I didn't know what I would find, I didn't even go to the station, just got in the patrol car and drove straight there."

"Why would he do that?" Lenn was covering her mouth. "That means he . . . he was turning himself in, because he had Tommy, right Morrissey?"

"Y-yes, I think so. Yeah, he hit me and then the next thing I knew he was standing there with Tommy in his arms, so I just assumed he had them in his car or . . ."

"Carl rode his bike to the goat shed, he had his license taken away last year for driving under the influence."

"But then how did Tommy get to the goat farm? There's no way he could ride a baby on a bike in the middle of the night—"

"Morrissey." Lenn shot me a withering look. Her face fell. She looked weak and was begging for me to save this for another time.

"I don't know how it all played out yet, Morrissey, but we'll put the puzzle pieces together, I promise you. All that I can say is, having known Carl since we were babies, he didn't trust anybody at the time he sent me that message."

Kel patted her elbow now, pulling a handkerchief from his pants pocket and passing it to her. She took it, dabbing the wetness as I watched on, something uneasy blooming to life inside of me.

"And I'd say he loved you 'til the end, Lenn," Kel continued. "I'd say he put you first, even if it meant he lost everything. His freedom. His life. *You.*"

CHAPTER FORTY-FOUR

Morrissey
Eighth day: 8.15 a.m.

"You know it's funny, I assumed when you came home that night you just forgot to turn on the security system when you went to bed and that's how Tommy got taken."

"Oh." Lenn made no further reply, only stared out the window as we cut through the early dawn mist of Smokey Hollow Road. I worked my splinted wrist, enjoying the dull pain from where I'd slipped out of the ties.

"I didn't realize Carl followed you in on the bike."

The car was silent with lingering questions. "Well, I don't know for sure, I didn't see him exactly, only heard Mom talk about it later like he had Tommy. She said it was so nice father and son were finally getting to know each other."

"But I thought he didn't have Tommy until after Spalding was dead?"

"And sometimes she told me you and Tommy were dead. I couldn't believe anything. She only wanted to say the things that would cut me the deepest in the moment."

"I still wish you would have told me about the night at the pool house, instead of going to Carl."

"What would it change?"

"Nothing, but at least I could've helped protect you before he descended into crazy town."

"I've been pulling away, I had it under control."

"Clearly not," I cracked, then regretted it.

"He was my best friend for all of my life, Morrissey, I couldn't just walk away."

"And it almost killed you and our son."

She pushed her head into her hands, a ragged groan on her lips.

"And your mom — how do you think she knew Spalding?" I pressed further.

"She said he milked the goats on the days Hank couldn't — he helped with odd jobs on the farm and always needed fast cash."

"And Carl?"

"She babysat him when he was little and she was pregnant with me. She said Carl was helping her with Tommy and she was so happy to finally get to know her grandson after we'd kept her away from him."

"She just told you all this freely while she held you captive in the lighthouse?"

Lenn tipped her head, eyes landing on me as we pulled up to the front gates of the Hollows. "What are you accusing me of, Morrissey?"

"Nothing," I replied, an unexplained sense of dread itching through my pores. "But why now? Why draw me out to the goat shed and give herself up?"

"She didn't give herself up. She was forcing your hand. It drove her crazy every day you walked free, all she could think about was more ways to send you over the edge, or to implicate you. When she had Carl drop files of Tommy on security camera, that wasn't to torture you. It was to plant evidence. It looks bad, Morrissey. They were all clues meant for Kel to find, Kel just never subpoenaed search warrants for our computers. If he had and found those . . ."

"But I didn't even think what I was seeing was real. The footage of Tommy only flashed on the screen — if I hadn't been in the kitchen, I would have missed it. I thought it was another nightmare."

"It was your own personal nightmare. She wanted you to trip up and incriminate yourself, she was so convinced I'd married someone evil. I think she was secretly wishing Carl would kill you once he found you at the goat shed — she was waiting just off the shoreline of the Hollows and it drove her insane that she couldn't hear or see anything. She jumped into action and hauled me out of the boat, dragging me up the shore and through the vineyard. She was going to kill you, I could see it in her eyes. She was so furious that what she thought were well-laid plans hadn't gone off as she expected. She talked to someone on the phone beforehand and all I can remember her saying was: 'Nobody will hear a thing in the goat shed.'

"I don't think she thought he'd bring Tommy, and I think she underestimated Carl's . . ." Lenn cupped a hand over her mouth. I assumed memories of her childhood friend in sweeter times were the cause of the sadness crossing her features. ". . . *love* for me. She thought his hate was bigger, but I just keep thinking that when he sent Kel the GPS coordinates it was because he wanted to do what was right. Deep down, he didn't trust her, and I think he just . . . lost himself somewhere on the way."

I let her words settle, heavy like the clouds that hung over the Point.

I didn't agree with her, I hated him and hoped he rotted in hell, but if the GPS coordinates saved our lives from madness last night, then I could learn to be grateful for him too.

For her sake.

We pulled through the gates of the Hollows. "Welcome home, baby."

It had hardly felt like home without her. It felt like prison, now that I knew how much Sheryl had breached our barriers without our even knowing. I'd done what I could, even followed Kel's suggestion to turn the security cameras in, and it had caused more harm than good.

"Be honest," Lenn said once I cut the engine. She stepped out of the Audi, "did you have a moment where you thought it was me that'd taken Tommy?"

I shook my head, slinging an arm over her shoulder. "I had moments where I thought everyone had taken Tommy. Even me."

Lenn chuckled softly as we stepped into the house. "I'm so thankful for your mom taking him for a few nights, I felt like I haven't slept in weeks. Let's just say I never want to see the lighthouse again."

"You want a drink to wind down? Might I suggest the Hollows red blend, a lush vintage to celebrate your return home." I opened the built-in wine fridge, sliding a bottle out and holding it to her.

"I'm okay if I never see another bottle of that stuff again."

I left it on the counter, then came around the island to hold her close. "I missed you. Do you want me to draw you a bath?"

"No more water, please," she laughed and my heart felt light again, like I might find that girl I loved deep down if I was patient enough. "Can we just lay down for a while? I kept dreaming about falling asleep in your arms. It killed me being so nearby, like the Count of Monte Cristo locked up on prison island, so close, yet so far. I never thought I'd feel you beside me again."

We collapsed onto the coach and I pulled her close. "I have so many regrets. Carl accused me of not protecting you, I know why now. I didn't, I didn't protect you. I should have checked on you, I should have slept on the floor next to your bedside that night if that's what it took."

"Morrissey . . ." she whispered, tucking herself under my shoulder.

"The pool house didn't even have a lock, Lenn. I should have put you in my room to keep you safe."

"There was nothing to keep me safe from, you didn't know."

"I should have. He'd been unraveling in the months leading up to that night. He was drinking so much, I . . . I should have realized—"

"People aren't themselves when they're in pain, Morrissey. I didn't tell you because it didn't feel like rape . . . it felt like a misunderstanding." She straightened her spine, eyes level with mine as they watered with truth. "I don't think he knew."

I crushed a hand over my eyes, squinting away the pain.

"I think he thought I was your mom." She was crying now. "He kept saying how sorry he was for ruining the family."

Salty pain tracked down my face as Lenn enveloped me in her arms, thighs straddling mine, cradling me against her as we cried together.

Every horrific moment, all because she'd been in the wrong place, at the wrong time, the night my father lost his mind.

CHAPTER FORTY-FIVE

Lennox
Four weeks later

Tommy squealed and ran into Morrissey's arms.

The little duck floats around his tiny biceps brought a wave of emotion over me. I was so thankful, never would I take for granted the light he brought me again.

"Ready for a swim, Tommy?" I asked him.

His toothless grin turned to me as he babbled.

"This boy was born a water baby, a little fish, the way he paddles in the water now. He's a stronger swimmer every day." Gigi smiled and patted her grandson on the back.

Tommy clutched the railing and bobbed in the shallow water.

I followed in after him, the warm chlorinated water tingling my toes and bringing a smile to my face. Tommy splashed and giggled, grasping at a pool ring before throwing it into the water and then paddling like a dog to chase after it. Gigi was right, he was a natural in the water.

"How's your dad feeling after his kidney transplant, Lennox?" My always-poised mother-in-law hovered above my shoulder.

"Great, thank you for asking. He should be here any minute. Today's the first day he's feeling well enough to venture out, he says."

"Oh, great, it's been so long since I've seen him."

"Speak of the devil," Morrissey announced, arm around my dad's shoulder as they came through the French doors and out onto the patio.

"Hey, Dad!" I waved from my spot at the pool.

Tommy started splashing, waving at his grandpa theatrically before going back to his pool ring.

Dad settled himself in the lounger next to me, a warm smile on his face. "How are you feeling?"

"I'm great, better now that all of the people I love most are here."

He grinned, waving to Tommy again as he swam nearer to us.

We were lucky to still have him — Morrissey had taken out a loan against Titan in the weeks before the abduction to help finance my dad's upcoming kidney transplant. It was because of Morrissey and Titan that my dad was sitting at my side and enjoying my son as he played in the pool right now.

I owed my husband more than words could say.

And I was more determined than ever to come out in the black with the vineyard next year. I'd already placed orders for different types of vines that may be a little more goat-resistant than the last batch.

Not that goats were really the issue anymore.

We'd all attended Hank Rockwell's funeral after my mother had stolen his life prematurely. He'd saved my son from Carl — that made him a hero in my book. Though I still wasn't convinced Carl would have hurt Tommy — some compassionate side of me thinks he only wanted to spend time with who he thought was his son.

Carl, the man who had gone from my best friend to my worst enemy. It still brought tears to my eyes.

After the funeral, the Monroe family donated a substantial sum to the downtown park in his name, a small poem engraved on a bench about legacies having a ripple effect on all the people we touch over a lifetime.

I spent every day counting my blessings now.

Kel had been pretty straightforward in reporting the updates about my mother's case — what he was able to, anyway. Security footage revealed my mom at the newspaper, meeting Carl, presumably to hand off the torn pages of my journal, or feed him more lies about my life to manipulate him into carrying out her plans.

Apparently Fawn and Kel were still fighting like cats and dogs — he served a warrant to my mother in jail, requiring her to take a DNA sample which would later match the evidence under Spalding Thurston's fingernails. They also found files of the original security footage from the Hollows on his personal laptop. Kel promised the jury wouldn't take long to deliberate on this — but Fawn was so adamant that her client was innocent, that she and Kel fought on the court steps outside of my mother's arraignment.

All of this information came to us via Kel, who was fuming mad that my mother had hired Fawn to represent her. A conflict of interest, he screamed. But we had no control over who represented my mother, and in truth, as Morrissey tried to explain to Kel, Fawn was always more opportunist than morally sound legal counsel.

Her trial was a media circus already and not even scheduled until next spring, but Fawn had already registered for various injunctions and delays as she built my mother's case — pro bono, of course.

And my father, flabbergasted by my mother's role in all of it.

I'm not sure how he didn't see it coming, considering technically she'd kidnapped me once before. Only then I was a newborn, and her connections with the sheriff got her off the hook. It's nice to think that maybe my dad just thought the best of her, even after all of these years. After two decades married but living mostly apart as if they were divorced, he still picked up her phone calls, still allowed her to crash on his couch for as long as she needed when she graced us with her wild presence, and he still updated her on all of the life details of her little girl.

From the beginning, Mom had been using Dad for information on my life. Even after Tommy was born, long after she hadn't been a regular presence. He loved her still, and she used it against him.

Compassion can be a killer.

Even when she'd returned to Thieves Cove and spent time next door with the goat farmer to gain access to our Wi-Fi and security, she'd called my dad on the phone with questions, pretending to be a hundred miles away. She'd even gone so far as to dismantle the security and sneak into the house in the days before the night Carl had taken Tommy, to steal the pistol in our nightstand and copies of some of the Titan paperwork in my office.

She was smart, far smarter than any of us gave her credit for. It took extreme circumstances for me to realize that my mother's skill wasn't in her mothering, but in her anti-mothering.

She tried to ruin me, and instead she built my resilience.

"Steaks, burgers, dogs, hot off the grill!" Morrissey called from the built-in across the patio.

I slipped into the water and swam to Tommy, pulling him into my arms and peppering his ruddy cheeks with kisses. "Ready to eat, sweet boy?"

His eyes focused on mine and clutched my heart.

So much trauma had surrounded the last two years, healing for all of us was my hope now.

"Hungry, baby?" I wrapped Tommy in a fuzzy towel and another around my own shoulders before slipping into the patio chair beside him.

Morrissey and Gigi brought plates of grilled food to the table. Tommy's little fingers stretched for the hamburgers.

"I know you two have been so very busy getting your lives back on track," Gigi said. "I've been wanting to do something to help you all heal from this. A gift from me so you can focus on your family. I've already talked to the attorney that handles Morrissey's father's estate, and I've made some initial deposits into a new account to take over the mortgage of the Hollows."

"Come again?" I nearly choked on my burger.

"And the business debt from Titan. They're strictly business investments, I know you have big plans and profit margins for the vineyard. If I can help, if my husband can give you this gift even if he's not here, it would mean so much. You're the most important thing to me, and I want to give the future generations of the Monroe family the best chance at a fruitful legacy for ages to come."

"Mom, that's generous," Morrissey attempted, "but we just can't accept it—"

"It's already settled."

"Mom, I sat in on the meetings with the estate attorney, there is no money — it's not possible."

"Honey—" she smiled thinly at him — "we don't talk about personal finances at the table. I'm merely giving my grandson a gift. You three need some peace, and I can provide it."

I covered her hand. "Gigi, please protect your future, I don't want you to worry about ours."

"How couldn't I? Besides, Morrissey's dad was very generous, he set up various business investments around the state and even a few offshore accounts—"

"Offshore accounts?" Morrissey frowned. "How much, Mom?"

She held up her hands. "It's impossible to say, I just come across things as I go through his paperwork. Your father's legacy lives on, far more than we even realized, so I want to make sure that's invested right back here at the Point with Tommy."

"But the pensions at Titan—"

"Oh, that's a separate business entity, honey. I don't know how that works, but your father was invested from Mackinac Island to Detroit and back again. I swear, just when I feel like I'm at the end of my rope, I say a little prayer and within the next day something just shows up . . . it's his way of taking care of us even when he's not here, Morrissey, I know it."

Dad shook his head minutely, another bite of his hamburger down before he turned to Tommy and began to play airplane with a stolen French fry.

My father, whose livelihood had been determined by Frank Monroe's business arrangements, took the high road, but I could see the sense of injustice bubbling under his skin.

"Thank Heaven for heated pools, it's getting chilly out here." I changed the subject, rubbing Tommy's back through the fuzzy towel. He smiled happily at me as he sucked on a soggy fry.

"He'll be wearing that little yellow hat I knitted for him soon," Gigi cooed.

"Oh, I packed it away. Every time I closed my eyes, I saw that flash of yellow floating in the dark water. It was haunting me. And ironically—" Morrissey squeezed my knee beneath the table — "that hat is the reason I knew for sure it wasn't Lenn that'd taken Tommy. It was too big, she'd never put it on him. Not yet. It had to have been someone that didn't know him well."

My heart ached that he'd suspected me at all, but I understood it — the chaos and public outcry surrounding the investigation was ferocious.

"Kel probably realized that," I mused. "Maybe that's why he didn't arrest you too — Mom was beside herself when every day you went free. She was so sure she'd masterminded this foolproof plot to overthrow the Monroe family."

Gigi's eyes held her son's, a sad smile deepening. "I can't believe the little gift I knitted for my grandbaby before he was born ended up being such an important detail in such an unexpected tragedy."

"Unexpected?" Morrissey scoffed. "It's not exactly the first time Sheryl's pulled this move."

Dad's eyes shot up, gaze landing on mine for a long moment across the table. "What? She took you? She . . . she was the one that took you to the boat when you were a baby?"

"Daddy?" I stood, sliding my arms around his shoulders as tears began to flood his eyes. "You never knew?"

"I-I knew she had issues, but I didn't think she had it in her to take you, not feed you . . . I thought a monster had taken you in a random abduction. W-why didn't you ever tell me, Lennox?"

"I didn't know until Kel did some digging in the reports. His dad had a file cabinet of paperwork at home they didn't open until he passed away, and . . . well, she did it, and because she knew Kel's dad, he kept it quiet if she promised to leave town and never do something like this again." Kel had also mentioned prosecuting a cold case as old as that one would be unlikely, but maybe the judge would allow it as supporting evidence for the current kidnapping case, or at least take it into consideration during sentencing.

"No," my dad gasped, horror written on his aging features. My heart went out to him. I'd always known my mother to be erratic, but I guess the fact that she was a monster was beyond him.

He loved her still. I could see it in the emotion hovering at his eyes.

So many secrets still separated us — his own with my mother, and mine with my husband. One particular morning came back to me, when I'd set my alarm for just after Morrissey left for work so I could drive to the student medical center on campus two hours away and receive a medical abortion. I'd smudged that memory from my mind before now, but the anxiety I'd felt driving home by myself that afternoon had nearly run me off the road. My fingers shaking, my eyes streaming, my stomach twisting with cramps, I'd aborted my baby because I knew no other way. Submerging myself in the bay had been the only thing to soothe away the ache left in my abdomen and heart then. The following day, with tears in my eyes, I'd swallowed the final pill at home and steered my course into a brighter future. Within hours the dull cramping had turned to violent spasms and a pressing headache, my vision blurry before I'd fallen into a restless sleep. The following morning, my future was sealed in bloodstained organic bedsheets.

I'd buried the evidence then, feeling I had no other option. Now, something inside of me wished I'd told Morrissey the truth from the beginning. But would it have changed anything?

I stretched a hand across the table to my father, so thankful that I had him and Tommy here, healthy and happy with me now. "I'm so sorry, Dad."

He wiped his mouth with a napkin before shaking his head and laughing ruefully. "I wish I could have been strong enough to see her for who she was then."

"Me too."

"You were a baby—"

"But she came in and out of my life after that, and I was so open. I let her in too much. Divulged personal things that I shouldn't have, told her so much about Carl—"

"Oh!" My dad shot up from his chair. "I almost forgot to show you something." He waved at me to follow him. He didn't stop until he reached the front door, his keys and a sealed manilla envelope sitting on the side table. "Carl wanted me to give this to you."

"What?" Just the name sent a chill through me.

"That night, before you were found — he must have dropped this off at the door. I found it tucked under my morning paper on the front porch."

"At your house?" I held the envelope to my chest.

Dad nodded. "I was so busy with the appointments for my transplant surgery it totally slipped my mind. But now that I think of it, Lennie, I think I played a part in all this without realizing it. Your mom used to call me up and ask all sorts of questions about you and Morrissey and Tommy, and I just chattered away happily, thinking she missed you and was finally doing the right thing, acting like your mom. Heck, I hate to say that I may have even done a little complaining about Frank Monroe and Titan over the years."

"A little?"

"A lot, a lot, but only because I knew that man had more tucked away than he let on. I had the keys to the warehouse when I worked in janitorial, I knew he had insurance policies on all three hundred employees at one time. I used my key to search the offices up and down after hours, looking for anything to prove the money still existed somewhere, just not where he said it was, but I never found a thing."

"Daddy, that's probably a crime what you did there, but it doesn't make a bit of difference now. When Mom has her mind set on something, you know how she is."

"I do, Lennie, and that's why I say I'm afraid it's a little my fault what happened to you. I spun those missing pensions and insurance policies around in my head for months, and I told your mother exactly what I thought about it on many occasions. Your mom even told me to ask you and Morrissey if you kept any Titan Transport paperwork at home, but I didn't want to bother you with all that just when you were starting out a new life together."

"Maybe that's why she wanted me to believe that Tommy and Morrissey were dead — she kept saying it and throwing papers at me, but they didn't mean anything. Copies of the title to our car and life insurance policies. I don't think she found the paperwork she wanted."

"No, I guess she didn't. It sounds like they were hiding offshore."

I gulped, realizing that in this case the Monroe family's triumph was on the backs of people like my father.

"And here I thought Titan went under because of bad business." He patted my shoulder. "I'll leave you alone."

I nearly crumbled under the weight of his vulnerability, thankful he understood how hard this was for me. Carl and I had been through so much, his last words to me were contained within and I wasn't sure if I was ready.

I rested the envelope on the kitchen counter, letting my fingertips run over the sealed edges before slipping a nail under the fold.

I had it open a second later, surprised to find only one single sheet of paper inside.

A photo with a date scrawled on the back. The dark slashes of ink indicated this photo was taken while Tommy and I were still missing, the night before the journals were printed. I traced my fingertip along the almost-familiar bend of the numbers. Was this Carl's handwriting, leaving me a message from beyond the grave? Or someone else with more knowledge of the situation than I knew?

I swallowed the fear lodged in my throat, and flipped the glossy photo paper over to reveal a grainy black-and-white security image, zoomed in multiple times. Goosebumps erupted on my skin as I squinted and brought it closer to my face to make out the people in the photo.

It was the parking lot of the newspaper, I was sure of that, but from a different angle — low and dark, as if someone was hunched in the shadows watching the exchange.

I held the photo in a ray of sunshine over the sink, narrowing my eyes even more until I realized I was definitely seeing Carl, the broad stretch of his shoulders and round face noticeable in comparison to the diminutive form across from him.

I groaned, realizing the person wore a hat, or some sort of hoodie to cover their head. Was this a photo of my mom meeting Carl — what was he trying to tell me with this? My eyes scanned the photo, searching for any other dominant details that I was meant to see.

Carl's Schwinn bike propped against the brick wall of the newspaper building, just like every day. A car parked in the foreground, blurry license plate catching my eye.

I could clearly make out the seven letters: *GMAGIGI*.

And then my blood ran cold.

CHAPTER FORTY-SIX

Morrissey

"Hey, gorgeous, whatcha got there?" I slipped behind my wife, planting a kiss at her neck in the kitchen.

"Just an old photo." She tucked an envelope into a side drawer and then spun, curling her arms around my neck. "Sorry I took so long."

"No worries. Your dad is on his second burger and Tommy is dominating the hot dog tray, I've got it all under control."

"And your mom?" Lenn asked.

"She's picking at her filet like usual." I kissed her softly. "Is it horrible that I can't wait to kick everyone out so I can have my way with you?"

She giggled like the schoolgirl I'd first fallen for, my favorite noise on this earth.

"That sounds so romantic." She froze for a moment, eyes casting over my shoulder. "Can we talk about turning the security cameras outside again? It feels weird, like someone's always watching."

"Oh, that was the point. I couldn't sleep when you were gone, but then I would go crazy, so I'd take sleeping pills, but then I worried that made me crazier."

"It sounds like you had an eventful time without me."

He shrugged. "The most miserable days of my life."

"Speaking of security cameras, did you ever check the gate camera that night at the goat shed? Just to see if any cars came down the Point? I doubt there's anything there, but since we know Carl couldn't have brought Tommy on the back of his bike that night—"

"I never thought of that. The fog gathers up on the knoll so much it's hard to get a clear view down the road, but I'll have a look later."

She smiled sweetly before kissing me once. "I love you, thank you for being the best man ever."

I shrugged. "Anything for you."

"BunBun! BunBun!" Tommy's voice filled the space a moment later.

"He can say my name now!" Mom chirped, Tommy on her hip as they danced into the kitchen in fits of giggles. "Say it again, Tommy, Grandma Gigi."

"BunBun! BunBun!" Tommy sang gleefully, then went to drooling on his little fist.

"You two are raising the smartest generation of Monroes yet; this little grandson of mine is going to rule the world someday."

"Well, not before a bath, he's covered in catsup." Lenn moved to take Tommy from my mom, but she resisted.

"Oh, let me give him his bedtime bath, you help your dad out to his car."

"Okay, are you sure?" Lenn held Tommy's bare foot, playing with his toes like piano keys and making him chuckle.

"Absolutely!" Mom kissed his cheeks and then turned, headed to the bathroom across from the nursery.

"Thank you for dinner tonight, Morrissey." Lenn's dad shrugged on his jacket and reached for his keys. "You kids call if you need anything, okay?"

"I'll walk you out, Dad." Lenn looped her arm in his elbow and they left through the front door.

I made my way down the hallway to the bathroom, smiling when I saw my son in the arms of my mother. She'd been through so much since my dad's death — no way could I tell her what really happened that night. I would die rather than ruin her last memories of her beloved husband.

"Still tryin' to wrap my head around your announcement at dinner, Mom." I settled next to her on the edge of the bath as Tommy splashed water.

"Don't think about it again, nothing will change. In fact, your rent at the Hollows will be cheaper than the mortgage on it because I'm going to pay Lenn a salaried wage to manage the vineyard. We can cut her a check from the business, or take it off the debt — you decide. Your father has made sure the Monroe family will be wealthy for many generations, and we can set up a trust for Tommy to make sure he's always protected."

"Mom, I don't know what to say . . ."

"Nothing is necessary. You and Tommy are the loves of my life now, I plan on taking care of you far beyond my natural life, Morrissey."

"But we've got a lot of debt. Just last week we signed paperwork to take out a loan against the future equity of the grapes to reinvest in more planted acres. She wants to market it as a tiny Tuscany in northern Michigan."

Mom's eyes widened, a frown crossing her features. "My . . . that wife of yours is quite ambitious, isn't she?"

"And industrious and hardworking, just a few of the things that drew me to her."

"I bet." Mom washed Tommy's hair gently. "I may not have created my own business, but I supported your dad so he could be the man he turned into. Your dad could be a hard man, but there was never a day that I regretted making myself a Monroe. If you walk the line just right, all of your worries can evaporate with a little cash and ingenuity. The Monroes have been set up to succeed, honey."

"We'll get Titan and the vineyard turning a profit again, Mom. Between Lenn and I, we've got this under control."

Mom tipped her head, eyes taking me in thoughtfully. "If that were the case, we wouldn't be here, honey."

She pressed her lips together, averting her eyes as I let her words sink in. Was she right? I'd been pushing forward on blind faith that Lenn and I could make this work, but maybe I was a fool.

"All of those big plans Lenn has for the vineyard," Mom continued, "they all cost money, dear. A lot of money. I've done what I can to set up you and my grandson from any further wacky stunts, but please don't let down your guard around desperate people — they do desperate things, Morrissey. Some families will do desperate and shameless things to acquire what they don't have."

She paused, washing Tommy sweetly under his little arms, then wringing out the wash rag before catching my eyes and smiling. "Sometimes it's more effective to replace a squeaky wheel than give it more oil, honey."

CHAPTER FORTY-SEVEN

Morrissey

My mother's statement about squeaky wheels was still rambling through my head as I kissed her goodbye later that night. With Tommy snuggled sweetly in bed with his blanket, I meandered through the suddenly empty house. Lenn had already picked up the few dishes from dinner, the soft notes of slow piano music tumbling through the sound system the only sound now.

I paused, catching sight of her curled in a blanket on the back porch, writing in her journal quietly as mist rolled over the bay beyond. I wondered again what my mother had meant — if she was implying that Lenn had invested too much in the wine business, or if she was musing about something else entirely.

I snagged a bottle of the Hollows red blend off the counter, opening it and pouring two large glasses. I sipped one, thankful for the warmth that hummed through my bloodstream, before easing out of the French doors and setting Lenn's glass on the railing at her side.

"Thank you," she whispered softly, eyes turned up to meet mine. "I was thinking about Kel and the papers he found about my case in his dad's things." She doodled tiny flowers in the corner of her journal pages as she spoke. "You've known Kel since middle school, when you moved to Thieves Cove, right?"

"Yeah."

"And you said he's older than you, but was held back in school."

"Sure."

"So that would make him around a year old when I was born?"

I thought back to Kel's birthday parties every year. "Almost two years, you're a little younger than me."

I was teasing, but the pensive look on her features told me she wasn't. "And Kel never knew his mom? She just handed over custody to his dad from day one?"

"That's what he said," I replied.

"Call me crazy, but do you think . . . is it possible that Kel and I have the same mom?"

I recoiled at the thought. "Really? That seems out there."

"Yeah . . ." she murmured. "But does it though?" She tapped her pen on the paper. "It was a big joke when we were young that my mom and Kel's dad dated right before she met and married my dad, so . . ."

"Lenn . . ."

She frowned softly, then seemed to relax and tipped her chin to me with a soft smile. "Who knows, who cares, right?"

"I-I guess?" I scratched my head, wondering now if the timelines did in fact line up. "It would maybe help explain why Kel's dad let your mom off after she took you."

"Yeah. It would."

Moments stretched long and slow, only the wind breaking the silence.

"Do you think Kel's ever thought about that?" I finally ventured.

"Would you?"

I thought about it, wondering if I would wonder about my mother's whereabouts if she'd abandoned me at birth. "No."

She nodded. Back to doodling in the margins.

"I'm going to work on some stuff in the office. Find me when you're done, okay?" I tipped her chin up, kissing her softly before I left her to her writing and slinked back through the house.

I reached the office, glimpsing the security camera I'd mounted at the corner to capture the hall and Tommy's room. I flipped the camera off on one side and then sat in the office chair.

I nudged the mouse and the computer screen came to life.

I sipped my wine again, still processing the news that my mother wanted to take over all the debt for the Hollows and Titan and give us a fresh start. I was blessed to be born a Monroe, I'd never doubted that, but sometimes the burden of the family obligations weighed heavy.

I couldn't help feeling that with my mother in control, both businesses would spin off in a new direction, with or without me.

I remembered then that Lenn had requested I pull the security footage that night. I clicked over to the file that kept track of the surveillance, clicking on the folder that was dated September.

The camera mounted at the gate was an older model and didn't take live video, only screen captures every thirty seconds. It only captured live videos when a motion detector near the gate was triggered.

It was these files that Sheryl had had access to via our Wi-Fi network — I'd since changed the password, but even then we'd been password-protected before and it had only taken a tech-savvy stranger with some motive to gain access to the inner workings of our life.

That thought sent a shiver scurrying down my spine.

I scrolled through the files, realizing then that I hadn't checked the gate footage that night, and it had been a mistake not to. First, a video was triggered just after ten o'clock. I maximized the window and hit play.

A stranger came on screen first, hooded but clearly small of frame. There wasn't much to see, but I caught sight of a hoof and a wet nose over the course of a small scuffle, before I realized it must've been Sheryl trying to trigger the alarm with the goat that night.

The video played while the animal wiggled and tried to break itself free, and it wasn't two minutes later that I showed up, untangling the baby goat and setting the grape masher above and out of range of the camera.

A few minutes later, a disturbance triggered the camera again, but nothing was visible on screen, and the camera flickered off again.

I frowned, realizing I would have to turn this footage in to Kel now for the prosecution's case against Sheryl.

I couldn't believe, at this very moment, Tommy's grandmother sat in jail for his kidnapping.

I continued to scroll through thumbnails of the stills that followed, zooming in as the timestamps moved closer to the time that Carl and Tommy showed up at the goat farm.

The road was dark and mist was clinging to the edges of the camera, but the shot down the driveway and out to the edge of Smokey Hollow Road was surprisingly clear.

I scrolled through a few more images, leaning closer to try to catch a glimpse of any activity in the far background of the screen where I figured the goat farmer's driveway must start.

Darkness, perpetual darkness, swallowed the grainy pixels.

I scrolled quickly, heart rate picking up as I tried to imagine how many minutes had gone by before I was tied up and Tommy was in Carl's arms standing among the goats.

Dark, lingering shadows stretched across the screen from the pine trees as the angle of the moon shifted. The mist clung heavier, the wind carried it away, and thirty-second timestamp by thirty-second timestamp I watched that night unfold from a new point of view.

And then I saw it.

Headlights.

I swallowed, leaning closer. Zooming tighter. The next photo was only a flash of the back end of the car. A light blurred part of the license plate, but the seven letters were clear: *GMAGIGI.*

A flashback of the very same vanity plate crossed my vision as ice chugged through my veins.

My mother held it up at the Fourth of July barbecue, announcing to everyone she had a new title: *Grandma Gigi.*

"No."

The possibilities flowed like lava through my mind. How hadn't Kel subpoenaed this already? And what was my responsibility in this instance?

I thought of all the gifts my mother had bestowed on Tommy and the provisions she'd made for his future — our future — and I thought of her words about squeaky wheels.

No way did she have it in her — no way did the kindest, most giving woman I knew, have it in her to . . . to what?

Take down our lives?

"Hey there," Lenn chimed from the doorway, one arm against the door jamb and her silky robe gaping open.

I swallowed, processing too much, fight or flight tensing my muscles.

I did the only thing then I knew how to do.

My fingers found the keys automatically, freedom from the truth on the other side of three taps.

Control. A. Delete.

The files I'd just been reviewing vanished in a flash.

"Did you find anything on the security cameras from that night?" Lenn came closer, the look in her eyes soft and lingering.

"Nope," I breathed as she reached me, her hands whispering along my shoulders and then crawling into my lap. Her legs straddled me, lips finding mine as she moved against me.

My hands came to her waist, my fingers lost against her silky skin.

"Good."

With her here, I could let bygones be bygones. With all of the evidence mounted against Sheryl, Kel didn't need mine. And as for that license plate, well . . . I can't be held responsible for what I didn't see.

"I love you so much. Thank you for always taking care of us," Lenn cooed at my ear, one hand crawling under my t-shirt to graze my chest. "We never talked about it, but after everything . . . you know Tommy is ours, right? I see your eyes and the sweet bow of your lips when I look into his little face. I just hope you don't think — well, maybe we could get a paternity test if you think there's a chance he's not yours."

"I don't need it. The results wouldn't matter anyway. Tommy is mine, you are mine. You're my family, the only thing that matters to me is right under this roof."

"Good," she purred, hips raking against mine seductively. "Because you're going to be a daddy again."

"Lenn, really?" I held her at arm's length, gaze traveling from her stomach back to her pretty eyes. "Another baby?"

Happy tears hovered at her eyes. "I just found out this morning. I thought . . . I thought for so long I was broken — first the miscarriage before Tommy and then all of those nights in that cold wet lighthouse. I thought Tommy would be all we would have and he would always be enough. But we've been blessed, this baby is our miracle baby."

"I can't believe it, a little brother or sister for Tommy." I held her close, pressing tender kisses to her temple. "Another Monroe. Gigi will be so proud."

CHAPTER FORTY-EIGHT

Gigi

How easy it is to manipulate desperate people with the thing they think they want most.

A wry grin turned my lips as I appreciated my new investment from the rear-view mirror. It had been a long time coming. I saw the writing on the wall all those years ago when Frank had started coming home from the yacht club with the scent of cheap-tart perfume on his collar and vodka on his lips.

My husband was a brilliant man when I married him, but not half as brilliant as his father and with none of the dogged determination.

But what my husband lacked, I made up for tenfold.

I knew which business to keep my nose out of, and which to turn my eye to. I knew my place, and it wasn't in the kitchen.

I'd more than won the lottery the day I married into the famous Monroe family, tycoons in the heydays of Motor City. Industry had dwindled to a fraction, and when the last factory closed up shop, Frank had been hellbent on getting away from it all up here, in the tiny little arctic armpit of Michigan.

Between two bays and a million miles away, as the Thieves Cove welcome sign proclaimed.

It made me sneer every time.

I'd done my duty for a while, until I saw my husband driving the last of his family's wealth into the ground.

It was then I'd had to make my stand.

But men don't often respond to words, it's actions that get them moving.

I eased around the bluff on Smokey Hollow Road, taking my time as fog shrouded the evergreens and clung to the cliffs.

The air felt sinister, black and cold and unforgiving.

I hated coming up to the Point, hated even more that my son was married to a woman that would most likely repeat her family's own tragic cycles and draw my family into her low-level swamp.

I'd begged Morrissey not to marry Lennox so quickly, begged him not to use the small stash of inheritance money I'd managed to squirrel away in a trust for him on the Hollows. I appreciated the extravagant wedding gift, I just didn't appreciate its recipient.

Lenn's plans to overhaul the Hollows and re-establish the vineyard were hopeless dreams at best, too similar to Frank's misguided attempts at establishing Titan, before he ran it into the ground with booze and boats and bimbos.

Lenn had already cost my son so much — a mansion, a sinking wine business, a father-in-law that needed payment upfront for a kidney surgery that would probably only prolong his life a questionable amount of years, where he would fill his trailer with cigarette smoke, debt, and failed dreams.

When Sheryl brought the journals to me that night, I hadn't thought much of the grand consequences; I hadn't even thought they'd affect my grandson. I'd only seen an opportunity.

Just as Lennox had seen one in my son.

It had taken me exactly two minutes of skimming the pages of the most incriminating of Lenn's journals before I realized I had to protect my husband — protect his legacy.

I knew then, there could be more evidence that would come to surface later that Tommy was my husband's, that Lenn could blackmail the Monroe family far into the future if she carried on her own family legacy of vile scheming and vapid desperation.

And proof in the court of public opinion is all that matters.

Lenn planted the scheme for me — it was there in her dark, haunted scrawl. Carl would be the key. I had to plant the idea of the affair publicly to divert attention from the reality — from my husband, from our family trust and the financial operations.

A town divided on one issue can't concern themselves with another.

I already had plans to sell my own home soon and buy something far away, maybe in the Virgin Islands, just in case someone like Fawn decided to file a civil suit against Titan. Morrissey was innocent, and with little to no control over the accounts — and I could ensure it stayed that way, without giving him enough access to hand his family's silver spoon over to his wife for the sake of grapes and wine.

A tiny Tuscany in Michigan.

I scoffed. Sheryl had brought the journal to me looking for simple blackmail — but I'd offered her one better.

I'd offered her revenge.

And, because desperate people always do desperate things, she was snagged like a fish on my hook.

A well-placed clue about Carl and a small but sizable initial payout with the promise for more was all it took to set a chain of events in motion.

I could have done better, in hindsight.

I could have hidden my tracks with a little more ingenuity, but I was proud of what I'd done — from the moment I'd started siphoning money out of the Titan account years ago and securing it offshore, to the moment Frank had realized that the pension fund was dry. I'd let him believe the fund manager had mishandled it and fled, but the truth of the matter was that it would now be the funds I would use to prop up the next generation of my family's legacy.

My long-term plan to save the family only required temporary collateral damage.

I hadn't expected Frank to kill himself in the end, but the thrill of surprise that had run through me when I saw him that morning shocked even me.

It's funny sometimes, how there's freedom in death.

Finding the bloody sheets that morning in the pool house bedroom had been a surprise too. At first, I thought Morrissey and Lenn had been together for the first time, and then I realized Morrissey had been in his room all night according to the house security camera. I instantly realized the little harlot had used her proximity to my family to seduce my husband and blackmail us later for money or media coverage or both. I knew then, she would only ever be a problem as long as she was in my son's life.

And then I saw the footage of Lenn leaving in the middle of the night, tears streaming down her face and t-shirt torn like she'd been pawed by a savage . . . I realized then that *she* was why my husband had killed himself.

Not because he thought he'd ruined the Monroe family name by sinking another lucrative business, but because he'd tarnished the wrong girl, stuck his business where it didn't belong.

My dear husband. So simple, so susceptible.

And unfortunately, he'd passed on this same trait to my son. My worst fear was that the prestigious legacy of the Monroe family would be tarnished if something insidious like news of a rape twisted the family tree.

And then my son had proposed to her on a whim, emptied his trust for the down payment on the Hollows, and then was planning a wedding and swiftly celebrating a pregnancy in close succession.

Fear had spiked my adrenaline at the thought of my new daughter-in-law carrying my late husband's baby — she may think she'd kept it a secret, but a mother always knows.

Even early in the pregnancy, while I'd showered them with baby gear and a nursery remodel, I'd planned ways to handle the baby if I thought there was a chance there could be evidence that he wasn't Morrissey's.

When Carl had revealed that Lenn had hand-delivered paternity papers proving Tommy was a Monroe, I'd known then the lies she was capable of — known that she'd bribed her lawyer to fake the documents, because the alternative was telling my son all the nasty details of the night she ruined the Monroe family forever.

Then, I'd been eager for vindication.

Lennox's mother had gone rogue from the start, conspiring with Carl to kidnap Tommy as well as Lenn that night, and then falsifying sexual misconduct claims to smear my son and the Monroe name. I'd had to sit and watch her pathetic game of cat and mouse unfold. I hadn't thought much of her idea, but I knew my son needed a lesson before he repeated the same broken cycles his father had, and that's why I'd delivered the important pages to Carl that night under the veil of anonymity. Morrissey would never rise to become a prominent figure in the Monroe legacy if he was too busy crushing grapes and battling paternity drama from his wife's lover.

He was better without them.

Carl deserved to know if Tommy was his, and Lennox deserved all the suffering for the scar she'd left on my family.

I hadn't known where the deranged woman planned on keeping Lenn, I didn't want details, but I *did* expect her to be talking sense into her daughter — making her realize what a life without the men of my family would be like.

Or else.

Desperate people do desperate things, and Sheryl wore the stench of financial ruin like the latest trendy perfume. It had taken only a few thousand to lure her into talking some sense into her daughter for a few days, with the promise of more if Lenn never came home, by whatever means necessary — a small price to pay to ensure that the family didn't bankrupt my son and the Monroe legacy in one fell swoop.

I'd been the one to tuck the tiny care package for Tommy in the dinghy — his baby-blue blanket he'd come home with from the hospital, a bottle, some infant formula, and cache of diapers. Carl had wrapped him in the little yellow rain jacket I'd left behind for him, so visible against the shadowy figure that shuttled the tiny infant off into the night on the grainy security footage.

And then, after watching with silent fascination as the nearest members of the Monroe family vanished before my eyes, I dropped the forgotten hat in the water and walked away, free of the last remaining evidence that could tie me to the disappearance of my grandson. That's why Hank had to die — his eyes all-seeing, even through the thickest fog.

I turned off Smokey Hollow Road, easing into the long drive that led to the bayside estate that had been our safely gated home for these last few tumultuous years.

I parked the car in the garage, walking through the door and into the kitchen before dropping my designer bag on the island and pulling the recorder from it. I plugged the charger into the wall, waiting for the familiar little blink, then worked the sticky tape off of my skin that was woven beneath my bra, around my underarm, and nestled right at the crook of my neck to pick up any and all conversations I had.

I sat down at the computer, pulling tonight's files from the recorder via AirDrop, and then hitting play as I listened to tonight's conversation around the dinner table.

Tonight, only a test run.

The real treat would come tomorrow, when I visited Sheryl at the Castle County jail and tried to gather sound-bites that could be edited together well enough to convince my son that Lenn had been in on her own kidnapping and the kidnapping of my grandson for the money all along.

Lenn had known from day one, I was sure of it.

I had confidence Sheryl wouldn't disappoint me; a mother just knows these things.

And a mother's love never dies.

THE END

THE JOFFE BOOKS STORY

We began in 2014 when Jasper agreed to publish his mum's much-rejected romance novel and it became a bestseller.

Since then we've grown into the largest independent publisher in the UK. We're extremely proud to publish some of the very best writers in the world, including Joy Ellis, Faith Martin, Caro Ramsay, Helen Forrester, Simon Brett and Robert Goddard. Everyone at Joffe Books loves reading and we never forget that it all begins with the magic of an author telling a story.

We are proud to publish talented first-time authors, as well as established writers whose books we love introducing to a new generation of readers.

We won Trade Publisher of the Year at the Independent Publishing Awards in 2023. We have been shortlisted for Independent Publisher of the Year at the British Book Awards for the last four years, and were shortlisted for the Diversity and Inclusivity Award at the 2022 Independent Publishing Awards. In 2023 we were shortlisted for Publisher of the Year at the RNA Industry Awards.

We built this company with your help, and we love to hear from you, so please email us about absolutely anything bookish at feedback@joffebooks.com

If you want to receive free books every Friday and hear about all our new releases, join our mailing list: www.joffebooks.com/contact

And when you tell your friends about us, just remember: it's pronounced Joffe as in coffee or toffee!